WANT TWO FREE EBOOKS?

Visit **nikikeith.com** to download *The Perfect Ride* and

The Perfect Daughter.

ONLY THE PRETTY ONES

NIKI KEITH

ONE

MY HAND SHOOK AS I GRIPPED THE KNIFE
tightly. It took all my willpower not to turn around and
use it on that SOBs eyes.

"Can you get her a slice of apple pie? She's never tried it
before," Kyle asked me, casually bringing his new
girlfriend into Lou's Inn. Of all the places in the world, he
just had to take her to the diner where I worked.
Seriously?

My sister was right. We had a knack for choosing the
wrong men. It had only been fifty-eight hours and twenty-
two minutes since Kyle dumped me, but he had already
moved on. Five months of my life, wasted. And for her?

I glanced back at the girl, unable to think of a good
insult for her. She was gorgeous with fiery curly hair, big
green eyes, and adorable freckles dotting her creamy arms

and legs. I recognized her from my precalculus class—Esme, I think her name was. This town was too small.

They sat in *our* corner booth, the one where Kyle and I used to share milkshakes during my breaks. Now he sat there with his tongue down her throat while running his fingers up and down her arm. He never kissed me like that. Maybe he just wasn't that into me…

My stomach twisted painfully as I set the knife down. How dare Kyle flaunt her in front of me after tossing my heart aside like yesterday's trash?

Their loud laughter felt like a dagger in my ears, mocking me. With a surge of betrayal burning inside, I pushed my glasses up my nose and fought the urge to take the whole pie and smash it into his face.

"Hey, Everly, what's wrong?" Asha asked, appearing beside me with her thick lashes fluttering. She looked past me and noticed Kyle flaunting his shiny trophy. "Oh, honey," she cooed, placing her brown hand on mine. "Let me take over," she said, handing me the coffeepot. "Table six needs a refill." She gave a playful wink.

My gaze moved from the coffeepot in my hand and out to the guy sitting at table six. To Finn Dunlap—an enigma wrapped in a blue dress shirt with a loose tie around his neck. His tousled dark hair fell into his gray-blue eyes that seemed to hold an ocean's worth of secrets. No one knew much about Finn, aside from his name.

Maybe it was time to change that.

I straightened my spine, pushing aside my hurt and humiliation as I grabbed a stainless-steel spatula to glimpse my pale complexion.

Asha giggled and snapped her fingers. "Work it, girl." She strutted away with Kyle's stupid pie order.

I ran my hand through my short, dark pixie cut, making sure every strand was in place before forcing a smile onto my tense face.

If Kyle wanted to show off his new girl, I could show him I had moved on, too. Sure, Finn was older and out of my league. But there was no way Kyle could compete with that, even if it was just harmless flirting.

I waltzed over to Finn's table, head held high, passing right by Kyle and what's-her-face. As I approached, Finn shook his hair from his eyes. "Hey there," I chirped cheerfully as I refilled his cup.

He nodded at me. "Thank you." His voice was low and smooth, like melted chocolate. But almost instantly, his gaze flicked back to his newspaper. His tousled front hair gave him an air of mystery, as if he had secrets hidden up his sleeve. I couldn't shake the feeling that those secrets were darker than anything our sleepy little town had ever known—and I was determined to unravel them.

I leaned casually against the empty booth next to him, my fingers playing with my apron as I asked the obvious question. "You're not from around here, are you?"

Strike one, Sherlock.

Finn merely shrugged in response, taking a sip of coffee and avoiding eye contact with me.

"Why Graybury?" I persisted, more like a detective than a flirtatious server.

Strike two.

Finn sat down his mug, and I tried not to squirm under the intensity of his stare. "Just passing through."

A smug grin spread across my face. Mysterious yet intriguing. "Well, it's always nice to see fresh faces around here. If you need anything at all, I'm your girl," I said with a playful squeeze of his broad shoulder. Stepping away from the table, I turned to leave, but then paused. "Hitchcock," I blurted out as an afterthought. Finn looked up from his newspaper, his expression giving nothing away. My palms suddenly felt sweaty as I continued, unsure of why I felt the need to keep talking. "You strike me as someone who appreciates the classics. And if you're looking for something to do tonight, there's this old drive-in theater on the outskirts of town showing a Hitchcock marathon."

Please be into black-and-white movies.

"Oh—no, I'm okay," Finn said before sticking his nose back into his boring newspaper, effectively shutting down any further conversation.

Strike… Just shut up already.

Sure, his rejection stung, but I wasn't leaving until I got *something* from my attempts. On tiptoes, I craned my neck to glimpse exactly what he was reading in the paper. SINGLES SCENE, the bold header read. Personal ads?

"Looking for a date?" I asked, and instantly wished I could push the REWIND button.

Finn shifted to me, his face flushing with heat. "I'm sorry, but do you mind?"

"Oh—" I sputtered, slowly taking a step back. "I'm just gonna… I'll be over there if you need me." I eased away from his table, my mind whirring.

The thought of him trawling through personal ads hoping someone would reply fueled an odd mix of emotions within me: jealousy, pity and—if I'm being honest—intrigue. Finn was drop dead gorgeous—how could he be single?

I slipped into the kitchen and took a sharp inhale as an idea popped into my head. Maybe there was a way for me to learn more about this handsome stranger.

Quickly grabbing Asha's wrist as she hurried past with a bottle of ketchup, I said, "I'm going to take a quick bathroom break, okay?"

Asha pouted her luscious lips and asked, "Oh no, did things not go well?" I sadly shook my head, and she gripped my shoulder in support. "Don't worry, boo, keep your head up."

Oh, I definitely would. Because I had one more trick up my sleeve.

Once locked inside the bathroom stall, I pulled out my cellphone and searched for Finn's profile. There was only one dating site locals used to hook up: MatchBox. Though I'd never been on MatchBox before, I knew of it through my sister Lani. She used to rave about how guys would go crazy over you if you posted a slutty picture of yourself and wrote something snarky in the "About Me" section. MatchBox was Lani's go to whenever she wanted to make a guy jealous.

Ha. Sorta like what I was doing now. I grinned smugly while swiping away profile after profile. With Graybury being such a small town and my search narrowed down by age, race, and gender, surely, I would find Finn if he was on MatchBox.

But after turning page after page with no luck, frustration simmered within me. I couldn't stay locked in that stall forever.

"Come on, there's got to be something," I whispered to

myself. My heart raced, and my fingertips tingled with anticipation. Yes, it was intrusive and borderline creepy, but this was an opportunity I was not willing to pass up.

I heard my boss, Lou, calling my name from the other side of the door. I quickly stuffed my phone into my pocket and pretended to wash my hands as I rushed to respond. "Coming!" I yelled back, flushing the toilet with my foot.

"Just in time. We have a family of five waiting to be served," he sang in an annoyingly chipper tone.

I rolled my eyes and forced a fake smile before flinging open the door. "All good now," I said, patting my stomach.

Lou, an older but energetic man, was usually not too bad to work for. However, when we were busy, he cracked under pressure. But then again, he had been running this restaurant for over thirty years, so he knew what he was doing.

I followed him out to the dining area and saw the family sitting at table six. I slammed into an invisible wall.

Finn was gone.

That night, the amber glow of the streetlights filtered through my curtains, casting a warm hue over my bedroom as I stared at my laptop screen. The idea of Finn having a dating profile lingered in my mind like an itch I couldn't scratch. So back to MatchBox it was.

Then, finally, I found it. Finn, in all his mysterious glory, his profile cryptic, hinting at a dark past and an insatiable curiosity for the unknown. A few generic interests and a single photo were all that appeared on his page. Nothing else.

Are you kidding me? My head tilted to the ceiling. But wait—Finn was literally just a click away from me.

I studied his features, those brooding bedroom eyes resembling Robert Pattison. He looked *so* hot.

My cursor hovered over the **CREATE PROFILE** button—my burning desire to contact him equally matched with a fear of rejection. One look at my boring photo, and Finn wouldn't bother responding.

My photo? What was I saying? Sixteen wasn't even old enough for a dating site. But they didn't have to know that…

I spun in my desk chair, my gaze drifting around the room, and then finally settling on a picture of me and Lani perched on my nightstand. The photo captured my sister's beauty perfectly: Lani's honey-blonde hair cascading over her shoulders, her almond-shaped eyes shimmering, and that effortlessly sexy smile that could make anyone weak in the knees.

"Maybe…" I whispered, an idea forming in my mind. I knew Lani had deleted her MatchBox account before going off to college. "There are bigger fish in the sea," she had said, eager to get out of Graybury.

I'd spent countless hours listening to Lani's stories of conquests and heartaches. I knew her like the back of my hand and was certain I could make her profile as authentic and believable as possible.

As I typed in my sister's details, though, I couldn't help but feel a flicker of guilt. But if using Lani's image gave me a chance to connect with Finn, wasn't it worth it? Absolutely.

Taking a deep breath, I began crafting the fake profile. With every detail I filled in, I felt my anxiety ebbing away, replaced by a thrill I hadn't experienced before. It was like stepping into someone else's skin, gaining access to a world that excluded me.

"All right, Lani, let's see if you can work your magic," I said, taking a moment to review the profile one last time before uploading it to the dating site. It needed to be alluring, and, most importantly, convincing.

Okay, that last bit was so me, but it fit Lani's profile just as well. The image I chose was of Lani standing on a picturesque cliffside, the wind tousling her hair. Her half Filipino heritage dominated in this picture, those gorgeous almond-shaped eyes staring fiercely into the distance. The background was a breathtaking mix of blues and greens, but it was Lani who truly captured the essence of wild freedom.

As soon as it went live, my heart raced with anticipation. Would Finn find the profile?

My mind was in a constant frenzy as I paced my room, stealing quick glances at my laptop. Possibilities flooded my thoughts, each one more exhilarating and daunting than the last. Would this actually work? Or would it all be for nothing? What did I hope to achieve from this risky endeavor?

A sudden ping broke me out of my racing thoughts, drawing me back to the computer screen. I leaned in closer to read the notification.

Some middle-aged, scrawny dude with a blond Santa Claus beard tried to start a conversation.

Ugh… I dismissed his chat and almost immediately, other chat notifications popped up. One after another, random guys attempted to connect with Lani's MatchBox profile.

"Are you serious?" I squealed, my finger clicking aggressively on the mouse to dismiss the lewd chat boxes. "I'm so sorry, sis..." I muttered, feeling a twinge of guilt for exposing my sister to such vulgar comments. Did guys actually think they could hook up with girls by talking like that? It was repulsive.

I shuddered and gasped, suddenly realizing something. If Finn was also on MatchBox, did that mean he had the same crude mindset? Oh god, I hoped not. I couldn't even pinpoint why I wanted to connect with Finn. Loneliness? It had only been *three days* since my breakup. Or maybe it was seeing how quickly Kyle had moved on that triggered me.

Rolling my eyes, I stared at the screen, the blinking cursor mocking me. The minutes dragged on like hours, each passing second amplifying my anxiety.

"Come on, Finn. Find her already."

I willed the universe to make it happen. I couldn't focus on anything else. The waiting game consumed all my energy. My fingers hovered over the keyboard. Don't tell me all this profile attracted were filthy-mouthed loners?

Maybe I should just message Finn first. But no, that would be too obvious, too desperate. Finn should come to Lani on his own terms. After all, I wasn't certain he'd even take the bait. What if Lani wasn't his type, either?

"Patience, Ev," I scolded myself, forcing my hands to stay still. After another twenty minutes, I got up from my desk chair and shifted to the comfort of my bed. Normally, I'd stalk Kyle's social media pages for traces that he missed me. But since seeing him with that girl, I wasn't sure I could take it. Not in the privacy of my room, where I could cry my heart out.

I couldn't sleep. The moment my head hit the pillow, thoughts of Finn discovering Lani's profile haunted me. And what he might say. My heart raced, chest tightening with each thunderous beat. It was maddening, the way my mind wouldn't let me rest.

Hours later, I gave in to my insomnia and crept out of bed. The moonlight cast eerie shadows across my bedroom floor as I moved like a ghost toward my laptop, which sat on my desk, mocking me with its silence.

With adrenaline flooding my system, I signed on to MatchBox, and there the new message sat in my inbox, from none other than Finn Dunlap.

Finn_D: Hi Lani

Two

I GNAWED ON MY LOWER LIP, RACKING MY BRAIN for a clever response, but Finn's three blinking ellipses were already taunting me.

> **Finn_D:** So, seek truth and report it, huh?

What? I uttered his words under my breath, trying to make sense of them. They seemed to hold some deeper meaning that I couldn't quite grasp. Frustration flooded through me as I wracked my brain for a clever retort. Lani would have effortlessly delivered a charming and playful response. But not me. I approached every interaction like a puzzle that needed to be solved.

Wait a second. The words truth and report clicked in my mind—something related to journalism, of course.

Everly, you can *do* this, girl. Just stop thinking about it so hard, and let it flow.

I glanced at Lani's picture, at her flirty, teasing nature. A broad smile spread across my face as I typed my reply.

I held my breath for Finn's reply. My palms were sweaty with anticipation when I saw Finn's three dot bubbles appear. But then they disappeared without a response. I straightened in my seat, my heart hitching to my throat.

"No, no, no."

What just happened? Was I not engaging enough? Did my text come across as too desperate? Ohmigod. What if I sounded… childish?

"I better give up now," I murmured, but then fidgeted in my chair as the ellipses started up again.

I squealed in excitement. A photographer. I never would've guessed. Leaning back in my seat, I gazed at his profile pic with new curiosity. His calm demeanor and easy smile suddenly took on a new meaning as I pictured him behind the lens, immersed in his passion. In that moment, I yearned for his camera lens to capture me as well, preserving me in time alongside all of his other enchanted memories.

But of course, that would never happen.

As soon as I saw the tiny heart emoji, my heart skipped a beat. It was a simple gesture, but it held so much meaning coming from Finn. He wasn't like the other sleazy profiles on MatchBox—he actually took the time to acknowledge and appreciate the details of my profile. *Lani's* profile, I rolled my eyes.

I swiveled my chair, the creak of its wheels echoing in the silent room. My fingers danced across the keyboard as I typed out my reply, unable to contain my genuine intrigue and disbelief at what was happening. We were actually connecting, two strangers brought together by technology.

In the back of my mind, a tiny voice warned me I was playing a dangerous game—after all, I was catfishing this guy. But I couldn't resist, couldn't stop myself from learning more about Finn and unraveling the mystery that shrouded him. Each additional detail made him even more captivating, pulling me deeper into the web we had spun together.

My giggles turned into a maniacal cackle as my fingers danced over the keyboard, fighting against my conscious to stop myself from digging a deeper hole. But the thrill of deception was too intoxicating to resist, drowning out any doubts I had. Finn wanted a date. That meant I was already in too deep to back out now.

Then again, I could do the right thing. But why should I? This was just harmless flirting, right?

I bit down hard on my tongue, resisting the urge to confess and cut things short. A scoff escaped my lips. Nobody was talking about forever or anything serious like that.

Without a second thought, I typed my answer.

The scalding hot liquid burned my hand, jolting me from my trance. "Watch it, Paisley," I hissed, immediately placing a washcloth over my hand to dry up the coffee and soothe the sting.

The afternoon shift at Lou's was in full swing. The sound of chatter and clinking silverware blended into a familiar background noise that paled in comparison to the weight of Finn's words from our earlier chat.

"*You* were standing in *my* way," Paisley, another server, snapped back, shooting me daggers before shoving the double doors open and heading out to the dining area with a customer's order.

Paisley was most likely correct. I might have been standing in her way, totally spaced out. The rush of adrenaline from my successful catfish scheme still coursed through my veins. Playing a different persona and keeping up the charade was exhilarating. It was both thrilling and terrifying at the same time. And Finn, oblivious to my identity, fell for every word I typed without hesitation. We stayed online chatting it up until six in the morning. And he had not the slightest clue who I really was.

He was so proud of an expensive camera he'd saved for, boasting about its impressive array of lenses and accessories. His love for photography radiated from him as he spoke about experimenting with different focal lengths, filters, and stop and shutter speeds. Though I couldn't fully comprehend all the technical terms, I enjoyed listening to Finn speak about his dream.

However, I'd expressed Lani's aspirations of being a reporter, chasing stories and uncovering the truth. While it was exciting then, today it'd left a bitter taste in my mouth. My true ambition, buying a used car, was a far cry from the adventurous spirit that seemed to captivate someone like Finn. I knew it wasn't fair to compare myself to Lani, but the conversation with Finn—someone more mature—had stirred something inside me, a desire for more, a yearning to be seen not only as the quirky girl behind the counter.

"Order's up!" the gruff cook called, hitting the bell, signaling me to grab the plates.

"Desire for more—yeah, right," I uttered, going to retrieve the plates of cheeseburgers and fries for table two.

"And can you refill the napkin dispensers afterward, Ev?" Lou huffed as he passed by, visibly agitated.

I sucked in a breath and plastered on my fake smile. My sister was out there living the dream in college, going on dates with fascinating, mature guys while I was here sulking from a breakup and weaving my way through hungry patrons.

Well, that wasn't entirely true. Regardless of whose

profile picture was there, *I* connected with Finn. My words held his interest. And now there was a date set up, my conscious reminded me. How was I going to get out of that? I could tell Finn the truth. That I'm just a bored, lonely sixteen-year-old with a stupid crush on him.

Yeah right.

"Hey, Everly, can I get an ice water?" a man called from a nearby booth.

I snapped back to reality and headed to the drink dispenser, trying to focus on work. But my thoughts kept drifting back to Finn. How I had gone from barely knowing his name to knowing his exact location in Graybury—off Willshire Road, down by the lake, hidden among tall oaks and ancient pines. It was a charming vacation rental, often used by out-of-towners visiting their families in this secluded town. This information only confirmed that Finn wasn't planning on staying in Graybury for long. He probably only told me his location in hopes of getting mine. But I could never reveal that to him.

"Everly—if you don't stop that, you'll wipe a hole in that table," Lou hissed, breaking my thoughts. "There are coffee cups that need refilling."

"Sure." I nodded, tucking the washcloth into my apron pocket quickly. I grabbed the coffeepot and poured the steaming liquid into cups without really seeing the customers. My gaze swept over the empty booth where Finn usually sat. A mix of disappointment and relief washed over me. I wasn't so sure I could face him just yet, not with that heavy deception hanging between us.

My attention snapped back to the task at hand. The aroma of freshly brewed coffee filled my nostrils. As I made my rounds, offering refills with a practiced smile, the sound of chatter and clinking cutlery blended into a comforting hum.

But then the loud clang of the bell disrupted the peaceful atmosphere as the door swung open with significant force. A disheveled, older Latina woman stumbled inside, eyes wild and panicky as she clutched a crumpled photograph. Her desperate gaze darted around the diner, searching for someone or something. With a sense of urgency, she lurched toward the nearest occupied table and thrust the photo into their hands. The customers shrank away in confusion and alarm, unsure how to react.

A hush fell over the bustling restaurant as all eyes turned to this woman. Undeterred, the woman shuffled from table to table, frantically showing the picture to each patron. Some shook their heads sadly in response, while others simply ignored her pleas.

Frowning in concern, I sat the coffee pot on an

unoccupied table and slowly approached the distressed woman—who babbled in Spanish with tears streaming down her cheeks.

"Mi hija!" she sobbed, jabbing a finger at the crumpled photo.

Smacking my forehead, I regretted not taking Spanish classes despite my mom's insistence that French would impress colleges. And well, you don't go against the county attorney, Sloane Baker, AKA my mom.

My heart clenched at the sight of the woman's defeated expression though as she moved on to the next table.

"Your daughter?" a brunette woman asked finally, while bouncing her crying toddler on her knee. Eventually, she shook her head regretfully, too.

The Latina woman shifted to me, her face a canvas of worry lines, as she staggered closer.

"Order's up!" the cook went again. I glanced back for Paisley to see if she'd grabbed the plate, but she was nowhere in sight.

A clammy hand clamped onto my wrist, pinning me in place. "Illiana," the woman choked, thrusting a picture of her daughter in front of my face. Illiana appeared to be in her early twenties, with fluffy dark hair and a radiant smile that could light up a room. I couldn't deny her beauty, but to my dismay, I had never seen her before.

It pained me to give this woman another no. "I'm so sorry," I said instead.

She gripped my wrist tighter. "Please…?"

"Everly," Lou barked from behind the counter. "The customers are waiting."

I shot him a furious look, signaling to the distraught woman with my eyes. Lou huffed a breath before leaving his workstation.

"All right, all right," he grumbled, splitting between us. He gently grabbed the woman's shoulders and ushered her to the door. "You're disturbing my customers," he told her quietly. "You must go to the police, okay? Policía?" Lou led her outside and pointed toward the sheriff's station. She nodded.

As Lou came back inside, she and I locked gazes through the window. Her fear ripped through me like a dagger made of ice. The raw emotion in her desperate eyes pleaded with me one last time before she spun away, as if finding her daughter depended solely on me.

THREE

WE SHOULD HAVE CALLED THE POLICE. THAT thought echoed in my mind like a distant bell after watching that poor woman at Lou's restaurant wither away into sorrow. What if she couldn't find the sheriff's station? Lou's scanty directions couldn't have been much help. It was terrible of us to just send her on her merry way like that.

My bike screeched to a halt on the gravel, sending a spray of pebbles skittering across the pavement. I'd almost passed my address. The house seemed to extend a shadowy arm toward me, beckoning me forward to act.

I dropped my bike in the empty driveway and rushed to Mom's emergency contacts on the refrigerator, where I'm certain we had listed the sheriff's line. My finger scrolled through the contacts posted—past the family doctor, a local plumber, Kyle's mother (barf) and bingo—

Sheriff Abernathy. Without hesitation, I took out my cell and dialed his number.

A young male voice answered after the first ring. "Sheriff's office, Deputy Fuller speaking," he said briskly. My mind blanked for a moment as I tried to gather my thoughts. What exactly was I reporting? I didn't get the woman's name or phone number or anything. "Hello?" The deputy prompted impatiently.

"Um, yes, I'd like to report a—a missing person," I said, voice small.

"A missing person?"

"Yes, um—" I closed my eyes, envisioning the girl's face, "a Latina, with black curly hair, dark eyes…"

The deputy interrupted me before I could continue. "Can we start with their name?"

I hesitated, mentally kicking myself for not asking more questions earlier. "Her name's Illiana, but I don't know her last name. Her mother seemed really worried, though," I added hastily.

There was a brief pause before the deputy spoke again, his tone professional yet tinged with youthfulness. "I'm sure she was. Can you give me any more information about Illiana? How old is she?"

"She looks young, probably in her early twenties—late teens."

"Probably?" He echoed my uncertainty wearily. "Do you know if Illiana was last seen on foot or in a car?"

I pushed my glasses up my nose absentmindedly, feeling the weight of his skepticism bearing down on me. "I don't know."

"Hmm... okay. Is she considered at risk?" His tone was serious now.

"At risk?" I repeated dumbly.

"Yes, is she pregnant or disabled? Does she have any vulnerabilities?"

My mind raced as I tried to remember any details that might be helpful. But I had only seen Illiana's photo briefly.

"Honestly," I began, feeling flustered, "I've never actually met Illiana in person. Her mother had come into Lou's Inn earlier looking for her, and she was very upset. I figured it must be serious if she was that worried."

He clicked his tongue. "Are you prank calling us?" His voice rose in pitch, clearly not believing my story.

Heat swelled in my chest. "A prank call? *No.* This woman is really searching for her…"

His line beeped. "Look," he interrupted, a sigh following. "If you see that woman again, either have her stop by to make a proper report or get some more details and call us back. I appreciate your concern, but I have another call to take." The line went dead before I could say anything else.

I stared at my cell in disbelief. *Fine*. I hung up, too.

But what were the odds that woman would even come back to Lou's? Clearly, she didn't make it to the sheriff, otherwise Deputy A-Hole would have had information about Illiana already, right?

I bit my lip and swayed against the fridge. "Well, I guess I tried," I spat out, my eyes lingering once again on Kyle's mother's number. Ugh.

I straightened and walked to the window, gazing at the garden that was Mom's passion project, yet she hired Benjamin Baxter to take care of it. Lately, the garden only served as a painful reminder of her absence. The bright mums seemed out of place and uninviting, reflecting my current somber mood.

As I drew the curtains closed, a shadowy figure appeared in the corner of my eye—moving inside the pool house. My frown deepened at the lurking figure stooped over and rambling about.

What the...?

A jolt of adrenaline surged through me as I headed for the door. I'd reached for the doorknob but stopped midair and grabbed the broom as a weapon. I clutched the broom's handle and ventured across the dewy grass with caution. The closer I came to the pool house, the dumber I felt for not grabbing something deadlier—like a knife.

What if it was a burglar? Or it could be Benjamin. Except he didn't work Fridays. Besides, he had no reason to go into the pool house.

I approached the glass door cautiously and tried to peer through but couldn't because the shade was closed. And the figure on the other side was gone. Was it just my imagination?

Confused, I slid the glass door open, slowly sticking my head inside. "Hello?" I whispered.

"Gotcha!" Lani jumped at me and almost made me pee my pants. As I gasped for air, she laughed and pulled me into an embrace that nearly squeezed the life out of me. "Oh, lil sis, calm down," she said, stepping back to pinch my cheeks. "No one's out to get you. Although if they were—you planned to sweep them under the rug?" she asked, arching a perfectly shaped brow at the broomstick in my hand.

I slowly broke into a grin. "What are you doing back?"

Lani flipped her long hair over her shoulder. "Well, don't look so surprised to see me, sis," she said, stepping outside and sliding shut the pool house door.

I hooked my arm in hers, tugging her closer, getting a whiff of her citrus scented perfume. "Of course, I'm excited to see you." I rested against her shoulder as we slinked back to the house. Lani looked great, too, in a handkerchief top and a pair of denim cut-off shorts with strappy sandals. Summer had just begun, and she had already achieved a full tan. I couldn't help my jealousy. Despite the sun's blazing heat, my skin remained as white as a ghost.

Lani and I had different dads. Hers was Filipino and had passed away a couple of years after Lani was born.

"I just can't believe you came home of all places for summer break," I said, struggling to hold my composure. I didn't expect to see her immediately after making that MatchBox profile.

A proud grin spread across Lani's face as she tucked her hair behind her ear in typical Lani fashion before bragging about one of her many escapades.

"Well, I had to come celebrate my win with you," she said, batting her long lashes.

"Win?" I echoed.

"I discovered a certain professor had been fabricating his research data to get more funding for his department. Anyway—*my* article exposed the truth," she said, jabbing a thumb at her chest.

A sharp gasp escaped my throat. "What was that like?"

"Terrifying. But a crook is a crook, and everyone

deserved to know the truth. And guess what else? Casey Maldonado noticed my article and invited me to dinner." She pressed her hands to her face and squealed.

I did, too. Casey Maldonado was an award-winning journalist from the city, who'd uncovered a huge political scandal last year. I couldn't imagine what it must've been like to sit across from someone so accomplished.

"Well, what did he say? Did he give you any advice?"

Lani's eyes dazzled as she recounted the dinner, dreamily. "Actually, yes. He called me brave for doing what I did and told me no matter what—never stop pursuing the truth. No matter how difficult or dangerous it may be. He said that's what separates true journalists from the rest."

"Wow." I breathed excitedly, impressed. I always knew Lani had the tenacity of a bloodhound when it came to uncovering the truth, and this connection could be her big break. "I'm really proud of you, sis," I croaked, throwing my arms around her quickly to hide my pang of insecurity. The only news I had was Kyle dumping me.

Lani hooked her arm in mine as we stepped in sync to the house. "Thanks, Ev. I'm still stoked about my article. I can tell you all about it over dinner. I'm starving. What did Sloane cook?"

It still surprised me whenever she called Mom by her

first name, even though Lani had been doing it all her life. I whipped to her once we arrived at the back door. "Take one guess."

"Nada," we said in unison. I stepped aside to let Lani into the house first, where she immediately made her way to the center of the kitchen and folded her arms in disbelief. "Same old Sloane," she muttered under her breath.

"We could go out to eat," I said, totally trying not to turn our reunion into a Bash-Mom-Fest, but Lani was already wrapping her beautiful golden mane into a topknot.

"I got this," she said, opening the fridge door, followed by a dramatic gasp. "Where's the meat in this house?" She spun to me in mock confusion. "Is Sloane on one of her crazy diet plans to impress some guy?"

"Ding ding," I grumbled, pulling open a cabinet to grab a box of pasta.

Lani rolled her eyes and dug inside the fridge, gathering an armload of vegetables. "Veggie stir-fry it is then," she said.

A short while later, the aroma of ginger, garlic, and onion sizzling in a skillet suffused the kitchen. Our laughter echoed off the tile walls as we chopped up a variety of veggies to add to the aromatics in the skillet.

"Remember that time you dumped ketchup into my chocolate cake mix?" Lani asked, her plump lips in an ear-to-ear grin.

I tossed a sliced mushroom at her. "I was six. And you told me to get whatever sweet ingredients I could find. Ketchup is…somewhat sweet."

"Is not." Lani laughed, poking me with a carrot stick. I stepped away from her, giggling, too, but my smile slowly faded. Ten-year-old Lani was only attempting to make me a cake for my birthday. Neither Mom nor Dad celebrated with me.

Lani glanced over and elbowed me. "Hey, that couldn't be me today. Not with the culinary skills Pierre lent me." She said his name in such a sultry way.

A boyfriend? Good. She wouldn't need MatchBox after all. My body relaxed a little. "So, tell me more about this *Pierre* guy," I said, mimicking her.

She flicked a piece of onion at me. "Enough about me. How's life as miniature Sloane?" She gestured to my pixie cut. "Is that some sort of statement?"

"Hey," I protested, feigning innocence. My hands flew up to smooth down my strands, self-consciously. Mom and I had recently gotten haircuts. "Don't you think it's cute?"

Lani stuck out her tongue and pretended to gag. "I

33

think it's sick." The knife hit the cutting board hard. "Sloane is trying her best to turn you into her."

I blinked at her in disbelief. "No, she isn't." I tossed a broccoli floret at her forehead.

Lani shut her eyes as the vegetable rolled down her nose and hit the counter. She retrieved the floret and tossed it back at me. "Is too. Why do you think she made you work at Lou's? That was her first job."

"Wrong. I'm working at Lou's, saving for a car."

Lani's eyes widened as she shimmied her shoulders. "Woo-hoo. Well, I don't care what anybody says." She shook her luxurious locks free from the knot. "I'm never cutting off my most prized possession." She whipped her hair across her face and struck a pose.

I backed away from the counter, pretending to have a camera. "Give me more, darling. Vogue. That's it. To the left. Chin up."

Lani struck pose after pose. Giggling, we bumped into each other as we got back to cooking. Although we were kidding around, inwardly, I admired how effortlessly beautiful Lani looked, even as she stirred the colorful medley of vegetables with a wooden spoon. She had a way of making everything seem sensual and alluring, from her flirty smile to the way she moved her hips while she cooked. My heart tore into two at the realization that was who Finn thought he'd connected with. It would never be me. I don't even know what possessed me to do something so stupid.

Lani had glanced at me to say something when a voice called out from the back door.

"I smell ginger," Gus Dearborn said.

I whipped to him standing at the back door, grinning at us stupidly. Gus was Mom's boyfriend, a total weirdo. Tall and thin with messy black hair and black square glasses. He always bared his teeth in a cheesy smile. He waved excitedly, that dumb grin plastered on his face.

"Ugh," I uttered under my breath, going to unlock the door to let him inside. "My mom isn't home yet," I said.

Gus entered anyway; eyes glued to Lani. "Who have we here, a chef? It smells yummy," he remarked, his eyes still roaming over Lani.

Lani's body stiffened as she stirred the boiling pasta. She shot me a furtive glance, subtly raising her eyebrows twice, our code for 'creep.'

She wasn't wrong about that. I suppressed my eye roll. "This is my sister Lani—Lani meet Mom's boyfriend, Gus," I said introducing them.

"Lani—that's right," Gus said, staggering forward awkwardly, arms outstretched for a hug.

Lani held up a wooden spoon to keep him at bay. "Not

over the stove," she said, stopping him in his tracks.

Gus flashed her two thumbs up instead, that stupid grin returning. "Gotcha. It's nice to meet you, still."

"Likewise," Lani uttered with a phony smile. Immediately, she returned to the sizzling skillet.

I dipped into his view, interrupting his mesmerizing gaze lingering on my sister. "Our Mom's not here," I repeated.

"Oh, that's okay. I can wait until she comes home," Gus said. "Maybe have a bit of that delicious meal?"

Lani turned around quickly, meeting his stare head-on. "Actually, we were kinda hoping for some sisterly time. Alone," she added.

Gus chuckled, throwing up his hands. "Well, don't let me get in your way." He headed for the door.

"We won't," Lani and I sang in unison. When Gus slipped out the door, I hurried over and turned the lock. I spun around, back against the door, erupting into laughter.

"What the hell does Sloane see in that guy?" Lani shuddered, making me laugh some more.

I dug into the half empty tub of mint chocolate chip ice cream Lani and I shared later that night. We were in the pool house, sitting cross-legged on the plush rug. Mint chocolate was still our favorite. Strikingly, it was the only thing Mom was sure to stock in the freezer.

"I can so eat this all day," I murmured, savoring the frosty treat.

Lani dug in for another scoop. "Agreed… Mm, finally, the news," Lani interrupted herself, leaving her spoon in the tub as she reached for the remote. The television mounted on the wall broadcasted the latest headlines. Lani turned up the volume, her eyes narrowing as she focused intently on the screen at the weather lady reporting warm temperatures.

"Lani—are you trying to plan your wardrobe for the week?" I smirked at her, expecting her to laugh, but she leaped to her feet and clicked off the TV.

"I can't believe this shit," she hissed, slamming the remote on the couch. "This town is so racist."

"What?" I blinked at her at the abrupt accusation. Lani ran a hand through her hair before plopping her hands on her hips. She stared at me, contemplating whether she should confide in me. I sat up straight, my face falling. "What is it, Lani?"

She shuffled to her messenger bag hanging on the coat hook. "I've been keeping records," she said, returning with a file folder. She lowered to sit beside me and spread the folder's contents for me to see. "These crimes are happening right here in Graybury…"

I stared at the newspaper clippings and missing flyers in utter shock. I hadn't heard of these cases before. The victims were all female, between the ages of eighteen and twenty-two. They'd found the victims in either ditches, rivers, or abandoned buildings.

Lani pointed at the clippings, her brown eyes blazing. "See? Barely a paragraph for each one. How are these stories not making headlines? The cops don't care because the victims aren't white."

My eyes scanned the contents once more, and a disturbing pattern emerged. Every victim shared the same feature: they *weren't* white. I shifted uncomfortably. "But do you really think the cops don't care? What if—?"

"You wouldn't understand it because you're not a minority, sis," Lani snapped. "*I* am, and this isn't fair. Racism isn't just hate crimes and racial slurs, you know. It's also the sneaky ways society values one life over another."

I nervously chewed on my lip, trying to recall if I had ever skimmed past articles like these in the local paper, never stopping to consider the tragedies they described. My head lowered in guilt and shame. "I see where you're coming from. It's just—this is Graybury, and Mom is like its savior. There's no way she would allow this, right?"

Lani scoffed. "Sloane hasn't been involved with the criminal justice system for almost a year. She's too busy playing everyone else's hero," she said with an eye roll. "Anyway," she continued, placing her documents back inside the folder. "I've been looking into all of this for my journalism classes. And it's…horrifying, Ev." She shook her head. "The murders are gruesome. What's even stranger is that the MO seems eerily similar to that serial killer Sloane put away years ago, Matthias Young."

I gulped. "The Graybury Slayer?" I whispered. Lani nodded.

More than a decade ago, six women fell victim to the Graybury Slayer's savage attacks. With each murder, he would take trophies, any personal item that belonged to his victim—an article of clothing or a piece of jewelry.

"It's not Matthias Young because he recently passed away. But I'm certain he has a copycat." Lani shifted to me, eyes wide with fear and fascination. "Some maniac determined to finish what Matthias started. This killer is taking trophies from his victims, too. Body parts." Lani dug her spoon back into her ice cream with renewed determination.

I couldn't even look at the ice cream anymore, let alone take another bite. The implications of Lani's words settled in my veins like lead. Body parts?

"Ev?" Lani called, waving her spoon in front of me. "I've come back to Graybury to crack this case," she gushed, her voice climbing with excitement. "I'm going to find out who this copycat is. And this case will jumpstart my reporter career."

Lani's voice faded as my thoughts returned to that Latina woman in the diner. Could her missing daughter, Illiana, be this copycat's latest victim?

FOUR

I SAT AT THE WINDOW BOOTH AT LOU'S, MY EYES fixated on the entrance as I took slow sips of my lukewarm chai tea. The faint scent of cinnamon and cardamom lingered up my nostrils, a comforting aroma that clashed with my anxious thoughts. It was early Saturday morning—my day off from work—but I was at Lou's waiting patiently for any sign of Illiana's mother. I needed to know if they were okay. Lani's words last night left me restless and on edge. The faces of those victims burned in my memory, their eyes pleading for someone to notice them, to care about their lives and deaths.

That Latina woman's fear and pain haunted me last night, too. I couldn't shut my eyes without wondering if something horrible was happening to her daughter at that exact moment.

So, bright and early, while shades of pink and orange still painted the sky, I hopped on my bike and pedaled to Lou's.

Every time the door chimed and someone new entered, my heart lurched in anticipation. But again, it was not the distraught mother. I felt I would never see that woman again.

"Still waiting for someone, love?" Asha said, appearing at my side. She looked like a teenager with her thick curly hair back in two puffs. Asha had been waiting on me for the past hour.

"Uh—actually yeah. I don't know if you heard about it, but there was a woman here desperately searching for her daughter."

Asha tilted her head thoughtfully. "Yeah—I think I overheard something like that from Lou. You know them?"

I leaned my elbow onto the Formica table's cold, smooth surface and propped up my chin with my hand. Thoughts raced through my mind as I spoke. "Not really. Just wish I'd done more to help, you know."

Asha nodded gravely, her dark eyes full of empathy. "That's understandable and all, but you're only sixteen. Every mystery isn't yours to solve, girl. Besides, maybe her daughter isn't missing anymore." She shrugged nonchalantly. "Can I get you a fresh cup?" She gestured to my murky cup of tea.

I shook my head, my mind still churning only with new considerations. What if Asha was right? Maybe I was overreacting, and Illiana was safe and sound. Perhaps that's why her mother hadn't filed a report with the sheriff. I realized I had automatically assumed the worst without evidence to support it. The growing sense of unease in my chest subsided at the thought. Maybe everything was fine after all.

But the bell jingled again, and on impulse, my neck snapped to the entrance. Was it her?

I lifted for a better view. Nope—just a couple of local farmers.

I sighed. Okay, this was getting ridiculous. I looked pathetic sitting at the diner on my off day, obsessing over the customers walking through the door. It was almost noon, which meant my awkward not-so-date with Finn was coming up. Unable to resist the temptation, I decided to spy on him from a safe distance. My idea was to appear as if Lani was running late before eventually sending a text canceling our plans. As much as I hated it, standing him up seemed like the only option out—aside from telling the truth, of course.

I gripped the edge of the table and got to my feet just as the doorbell jangled once more.

Ugh. "Happy Saturday to me," I uttered under my breath at Kyle and It Girl slipping inside the diner arm in arm. I exhaled slowly through my nose, starting down the aisle toward them.

"Hey, Ev—" Kyle said, tone cool and collected. He had that lazy smirk on his face, the one he knew irked my very last nerve. "Can you get our orders?"

Asha popped up beside me, pen and pad in hand. "Oh—Everly's…"

"Got this," I said, cutting off her sentence. I took the pen and pad from her. "What would you guys like?" I batted my lashes at them sweetly.

His girlfriend squeezed his arm tighter, as if claiming him as her territory. "I want a cheeseburger," she said. I scribbled that down.

"And onion rings," Kyle added.

I nodded. "Two burgers, and onion rings… That'll be…" I tapped the pen on my chin, feigning thoughtfulness. "Exactly none of my business, because I'm *not* your waitress today. Get it yourself." I thrust the pen and pad into Kyle's chest with a bit more force than necessary. My steps were brisk as I walked away. Unlocking my bike with shaky fingers, I swung my leg over the seat and pedaled away as fast as possible.

Maybe some would say I handled things rudely, but I didn't care. It was tiring being treated like a lowly servant by someone who used to mean everything to me. If Lou had been there to witness it, he'd probably run straight to my mom and snitch on me. But I couldn't bring myself to care. Kyle got exactly what he deserved for treating me like our relationship meant nothing now.

The summer sun beat down on the pavement outside as I stood behind a thick oak tree across the street from The Cupcake Cottage. The sweet scent of pastries and freshly mown grass mingled with the warm summer breeze, but I hardly noticed. My focus was solely on Finn pacing under the blazing sun, checking his watch. Again.

Just minutes after my arrival, he strode into view, dressed in stone-washed jean shorts and a form-fitting, vibrant tee that highlighted the sculpted contours of his body. The expensive camera he'd been using for his photo shoot still hung around his neck, a symbol of his passion. As he shifted his weight from one foot to the other, his piercing gray-blue eyes swept over the park. It was as if he could sense my presence without even seeing me.

Guilt twisted my stomach into knots watching him clutch a bouquet of wildflowers—intended for Lani, utterly unaware that the girl he was waiting for didn't truly exist—at least not in the way he thought.

He hopefully glanced down the sidewalk for Lani's arrival. I ducked behind the tree, trying to hide from my own actions. This date must've really meant a lot to him. Was I a horrible person? He didn't deserve the façade I'd created.

But I didn't want to let go yet either. Seeing him like this—so vulnerable and full of hope—made him even more swoon-worthy. The way his eyes flickered between scanning the area and checking his phone only added to his allure. He was like a character ripped straight from the pages of a romance novel.

My fingers dug into the rough tree bark as I watched Finn from my hiding spot. The sun cast dappled shadows across his face, highlighting the subtle curves of his cheekbones and the intensity of his gaze. He checked his phone and leaned against the bakery wall, more at ease now. He gazed down the road with a mixture of eagerness and patience, no doubt picturing Lani walking toward him in a sundress, her hair glinting in the sun.

I wanted to come clean and end this madness before it got ugly. But then he smiled, shy yet radiant, and my resolve crumbled. I couldn't bear to wipe that smile from his face. Not yet.

I gripped the tree trunk tighter, jealousy and longing coursing through my veins. I wished, more than anything, that I could be the one walking up to meet him. That I could take Lani's place, slip into her skin, and finally know the joy of Finn's embrace.

A car door slammed in the distance. Finn's head jerked up, eyes widening. I peeked at the woman emerging from a blue sedan. A stranger. Not Lani.

Finn's face fell, cheeks draining of color. He looked so small and lost, all the light gone from his eyes. The bouquet of wildflowers dangling limply from his hand.

I melted into the shadows once again, my conscious gnawing at my insides to tell him who I really was. I knew it wasn't fair to make him suffer like that. It was downright selfish, in fact. But he was mysterious and captivating, and different from anyone in this small town. And I longed to know him. With only the stroke of my keyboard, we were here. I had to know how much further we could go.

"Nice flowers, dude!" A random passerby called out to Finn, causing my heart to jump into my throat. The last thing I needed was someone to draw attention to him—or worse, to me.

"Thanks," Finn called back politely.

After a brief pause, I cautiously peeked around the gnarled trunk just in time to witness Finn slipping through the door of the quaint bakery. My eyes followed him as he gracefully took a seat at a small table near the entrance, surely with the intention of Lani seeing him upon her arrival. Only she wasn't coming.

Finn looked so hopelessly romantic, too. He stared at the bouquet in his hand for a moment, then carefully placed it on the table. The arrangement of wildflowers was so beautiful that my pang of jealousy returned. I wished they were for me.

Leaning against the rough tree bark, I felt defeated and suffocated by my guilt. The green foliage surrounding me seemed to close in, like a thick fog I couldn't escape.

Why did he have to be so sweet? And why did he have to bring flowers already? It only made my heart ache even more for what I knew could never be.

I bit my lip, leaning to spy on Finn once more. A nervous smile displayed on his face. I could see his shoulders hunching slightly as disappointment crept into his posture.

It was one thing to catfish someone online; it was another to witness firsthand the pain I was causing, however unintentional it might have been.

With a heavy heart, I pulled out my cellphone. The least I could do was put an end to this charade and spare Finn any further heartache. Taking a deep breath, I logged onto Lani's fake profile on MatchBox.

> **Lani2.0:** Hey. Something came up and I can't make it. Sorry Finn.

My thumb hovered hesitantly over the SEND button as I reread the message. It felt like a lie, but I didn't really know what else to say. It didn't dawn on me either how Finn might take the news.

But there was no turning back now—I hit SEND and immediately shifted my gaze back to the window. From my vantage point, I saw Finn hastily pull his phone from his pocket. His brow furrowed as he read the message, and for a moment, I thought I saw a flicker of anger cross his face. But a mask of palpable disappointment quickly replaced it. He glanced out the window for Lani one last time, still hoping she was coming.

Fear gripped me and I pressed myself against the rough tree bark again, praying he didn't spot me. When I dared to peek back out, I saw Finn's shoulders slump in defeat as he thumbed out his response.

My pulse quickened as my phone vibrated in my

clammy hand. The screen lit up with Finn's response, his words driving a fresh surge of guilt through my veins.

Aw. He was too sweet. I chewed on my lip while glimpsing around the tree, hoping to steal one last look at him. But he was gone. All that remained was the bouquet, abandoned on the table where Finn had sat.

FIVE

A SHARP KNOCK ON MY DOOR INTERRUPTED THE music in my ears that evening. Before I could answer, Lani barged inside and folded her arms across her chest, looking absolutely pissed.

Ohmigod—*MatchBox*. How did she find out? I sat up on my bed, pulling out an earbud. "Lani… I can explain…" I blurted out, pushing myself up against the headboard.

Lani shut the door behind her. "You're damn right you will. Why didn't you tell me Kyle broke up with you?"

"Wait, what?" I squinted in confusion. "*Kyle*…" Did she really not know about MatchBox? The absurdity of my panic attack almost made me want to burst into laughter.

"Yes, Kyle—your boyfriend of five months. Why wouldn't you tell me?" She came and scooted me over to climb into bed beside me, sounding genuinely hurt. She snuggled close. "I'm so sorry. Weren't you crazy about that guy?"

I shrugged, not in the mood to dwell on Kyle and his actions. All I could see was that stupid smirk on his face at Lou's. "Kyle is a jerk. And apparently, he's already moved on—there's not much more to say."

"He has another girlfriend?" Lani gasped, clamping a warm hand on my wrist. "Did he *cheat* on you?"

The thought never even entered my mind. When did he start seeing this new girl? Was that the true reason for our sudden breakup? Did it matter anymore, anyway? I needed to move on. "I couldn't care less," I spat out.

"Oh, hell no—is he still driving that red pickup?" Lani jumped to her feet. "We are so going to key the paint off that piece of sh…"

"Lani—Lani?" I snapped, grabbing her and tugging her back onto the bed. "I. Don't. Care."

She took a deep breath, dropping her shoulders. "Are you okay, though?" Her tone was serious as she studied me.

I couldn't even lie. My words would jumble, and she would instantly know I wasn't telling the truth. I just bobbed my head instead.

She wrapped her arms around me. "He didn't deserve

you. I don't care what downgraded skank he's got…" she said, but I rolled my eyes, breaking from her embrace. "Hey—" She clamped her hand on my shoulder tightly. "Look at me. You are a beautiful, smart, one-of-a-kind gem that any guy would be lucky to have."

Her words were so kind I couldn't look her in the eye. "That was really sweet," I croaked, gaze fixed on my quilted bedspread.

Lani kissed me on the cheek. "It's the truth, sis."

I frowned. "Wait a second. Who told you?"

"Sloane," she uttered, her face souring. "I can't believe she just left you to wallow in your heartbreak alone."

"It's not like that at all," I said hurriedly, unsure why I felt I should be defending Mom. "I told you, I'm fine. Mom shouldn't have to put her job on hold to wipe my nose over some stupid boy."

"Wiping your nose *is* her job. This is your first breakup, Ev. Did your dad come back to Graybury and check how you're doing?"

I shrugged. "I haven't told him yet. But he's busy in Wood River with his sheriff duties."

Lani rolled her eyes. "You know what—eff them both. I'm just glad I'm here for you. Now come on, let's go raid the fridge." Despite my resistance, Lani pulled me up and dragged me down the stairs.

"You know there's nothing good in there, right?" I reminded her.

Lani paused, cursing under her breath. "Right. Let's…order a pizza then." She snapped her fingers. "No, I've got it." She slowly turned to me. "Let's…have a pool party!" She grabbed both of my hands, practically vibrating with anticipation.

I squinted at her. "Are you crazy?"

"Nope. We will post it on social media and tag Kyle in all the photos, and it'll be the ultimate revenge." She tilted her head back and squealed gleefully.

"Lani, we can't just throw a last-minute pool party. Mom would never…"

"No, she absolutely will not," Mom interrupted me, entering through the backdoor. She tugged off her gardening gloves, eying Lani skeptically. "What are you up to, Lani?" she stopped in front of us, placing both hands on her hips. Mom was tall and athletic looking with a blonde pixie cut, and sharp blue eyes that pierced right through you. I thought she looked a lot like Sharon Stone.

Lani cocked her head in Mom's direction. "I'm trying—*going* to lift your daughter's spirits and her self-esteem."

"Exactly how will one of your full-blown ragers boost Ev's self-esteem?" Mom demanded, folding her arms.

"It just will, okay," Lani said, unable to come up with a better answer. "Besides, it's summer. Why shouldn't she have some fun? Or would you prefer she waste the summer away smelling bacon grease at that musty old diner?"

"It'll just be a few people," I finally said before Mom could say anything nasty. "And we'll end it before midnight," I added. Lani whipped to me quick, but I ignored her. "Deal?" I asked Mom.

"Fine," she said, followed by a sigh. She was about to say more when Benjamin tapped on the back door before sauntering into the kitchen.

His brown, muscular arms glistened with sweat. He carried a basket of freshly trimmed hedge clippings. His dark eyes lit up at me as we shared a private smile. Benjamin was strikingly handsome—clean cut, all sharp angles and smooth, dark skin, with a lean but chiseled frame. He had these adorable facial markings like splashes of freckles on his cheeks and nose, and a tiny hoop earring in his left ear. I'd developed an unspoken crush on him. But Benjamin was twenty-one, and as usual, I didn't stand a chance.

"Ms. Baker—I finished up trimming the bushes out front," he said, gesturing to the basket. "Thought I'd bring these in for compost."

Lani cleared her throat loudly. I glanced at her, practically devouring Benjamin with her eyes. She extended her hand for Benjamin to shake. "I don't believe we've met," she said. Their fingers lingered for a moment too long, and I couldn't ignore the pang of jealousy coursing through my veins. Lani was so lucky.

Benjamin licked his lips, struggling to gather his words.

"Lani, Benjamin is my handy helper," Mom said, stepping up beside her to get her attention. "Now, if you don't mind, he'd like his hand back to continue doing his job." Her eyes landed on Benjamin sternly when she said the last part.

He quickly slipped his hand free of Lani's, his smile retreating. "Yes, ma'am," he uttered, forcing a playful salute. He nodded at Lani and me and went outside with his basket.

"Now this party—" Mom said. "I don't want any nonsense, Lani. If the neighbors feel they need to call the police…"

"Mighty Sloane will pull some strings and get her daughters out of trouble, am I right?" Lani grinned smugly.

Mom shook her head, uttering curses under her breath while going back out to her garden. My eyes widened at Lani in disbelief she just said that.

"What?" Lani feigned innocence. She clutched my hands again, forcing me to bounce around in circles with her. "We're having a par-ty. We're having a par-ty."

Barely an hour later, the party was in full swing. Strobe lights flashed across the inky water of the pool, music blared from giant speakers, and strangers milled about the yard, red cups in hand.

Lani had abandoned me to mingle with her friends, leaving me leaning against the snack table and surveying the crowd. Guests trickled in and filled the backyard with laughter and conversation. Not a care in the world about what the party was for.

I fidgeted with the strap of my red, one-piece swimsuit, glancing around nervously. So much for boosting my self-esteem. I felt like a giant Twizzler compared to Lani, who was rocking a cheetah-print bikini under a sheer cover up that hugged her curves. Her hair was up in a sleek bun. She wore gold bracelets that jangled with each movement. I couldn't help but feel inadequate next to her. She was like a goddess.

Sighing miserably, I plucked a grape from a stem in a bowl on the table and popped it into my mouth, and nearly choked on it at the sight of Benjamin, shirtless and sculpted muscles as he filled a tin bucket with more ice. He glanced up and spotted me and broke into a grin.

Oh no, my brain screamed as he came over in a pair of navy-blue trunks.

"Hey," Benjamin called over the thumping techno bass. I nodded awkwardly, pushing my glasses off my nose. "It's nice to see a familiar face," he shouted.

"Agreed," I called back, with a hand cupping my mouth.

"So, you won't believe what I found…" he began, just as Lani sashayed over to him.

"Are you boring my sis, pool boy?" Her taunts carried over the music. Benjamin folded his arms across his chest, and the muscles in his arms flexed. Lani stalked around him, swaying gracefully to the music, continuing her teasing. "We don't want to hear about the algae blooms this time of year, pool boy."

I didn't get it. Why was she picking on Benjamin? I thought she liked him.

She poked his chest with a French tipped nail. I shifted uncomfortably, searching Benjamin's face. He sucked his teeth, a deep dimple forming in his cheek as he caught Lani's wrist just as she fixed to poke him again. He held her close and murmured something in her ear, causing her cheeks to fill with warmth. Whatever he had said threw Lani off-balance. Blushing profusely, she adjusted her hair to make sure it was all in its rightful place. After Benjamin let go of her wrist and smiled contentedly, he headed off. But not before his and Lani's pinky fingers intertwined in a silent exchange. Clearly something meant for only them, yet I stood there observing it all like a complete creep.

I twirled to face the table, pretending to be busy and knocked over a stack of cups.

"So, having fun?" Lani squealed, coming up and throwing her arms around me, as if she and Benjamin totally did not just do… whatever that just was…

And did she say fun? I silently wished that the night was over already. But then I blinked at Lani, at the eagerness in her eyes. She genuinely wanted me to enjoy myself. After all, she put all this together at the last minute for me, and the party was a hit. The least I could do was show my gratitude. My smile broadened. "Absolutely. Thank you, Lani," I said, squeezing her tight.

"Good. Now let's tag Kyle in that picture." She whipped out her phone. "Say sisters!" On impulse, we struck a back-to-back pose, arms raised, and all pouty lips. Her phone flashed a couple of times, and we laughed ridiculously as she uploaded them.

"Eat your heart out, Kyle. Now, let's dance!" She hooked her arm in mine, and we went to the makeshift dance floor near the patio. As we bounced to the upbeat rhythm, an attractive, blue-eyed, dark-haired guy stared in our direction. I stepped back so that he could go to Lani if he wanted. But Lani took my hand and tugged me forward. "Uh-uh, he wants to dance with you," she said, eyes beaming, egging me on. "Go get em' sis!" She gave me an encouraging shove toward him.

"I'm Mark," the guy said, eyes crinkling when he smiled at me.

I gave a tiny wave. "Everly."

He grabbed my hand, skillfully twirling me around like a seasoned dancer. I couldn't help but giggle in delight. With a playful shove and a gentle tug, he led me in a flawless rhythm to the music. Our bodies moved together effortlessly, lost in the moment. I briefly scanned behind me for Lani, but she was nowhere to be found.

After a couple more dances, Mark leaned forward, his breath hot on my neck. "Let's go somewhere quieter and talk."

"Um…" I hesitated, but his warm hand was already inside of mine, leading me through the mass of writhing bodies. I searched for Lani or Benjamin even—someone to interrupt us.

Mark chuckled, picking up his pace as if it were an exciting game to get to seclusion. He rushed up to the pool house, wide open because Lani allowed the guests to use the bathroom.

Mark squeezed my hand tighter, going over and plopping on the couch, pulling me on top of him. "Whoa!" We both cried in unison, me uttering nervous laughter. I quickly tried to climb off him, but he wrapped a powerful arm around my waist. "It's okay—you're hot," he said. His breath was hot against my earlobe and reeked of booze. When his hands pawed all over my body, groping and squeezing, I cringed.

"Okay—that's enough," I said, squirming to get out of his grip. Chuckling, he effortlessly lifted me and swapped our positions—putting me underneath him and hovered over me like a vulture on prey.

SIX

PANIC FLOODED MY VEINS AS HIS HEAVY BODY pressed down on mine, every ounce of me desperate to escape his cruel grasp. I couldn't feel my legs.

Mark held my arms over my head, interlacing his fingers with mine. He grasped my hands so tightly it was like a bear trap. His tongue was hot against my skin as he fiercely sucked my neck.

"Ow," I squeaked, wincing in pain.

"Mark!" Lani's voice was shrill. "What the hell are you doing? Get off her!" She tugged Mark up roughly by his hair. Lani went berserk on Mark, pounding him with closed fists. Though her feeble attempts did minor damage, it was enough to get Mark off me. He tumbled off the couch onto the floor. Once my legs were free, I hugged my knees to my chest, suddenly self-conscious in my bathing suit.

"Stop it—you crazy bitch," Mark hissed, shoving Lani. She yelped, stumbling backward, and falling over the coffee table.

I gasped, rushing to Lani's aid. "Are you okay?" I held out my hands to help her up. She reluctantly accepted.

Benjamin appeared, grabbing a fistful of Mark's shirt. "Get the hell out of here. Now." He practically dragged Mark toward the door, tossing him out like the trash he was. Benjamin went out behind Mark, ensuring that he would leave.

Lani shook her head, eyes clouding. "This is all my fault. I'm so sorry, Ev. What if…?" Her lip trembled, unable to finish.

"No—no, I'm okay." I clutched her in a tight embrace. "I'm all right," I repeated. Lani sniffled.

Benjamin returned, out of breath. "He's gone. Everyone okay?" His dark eyes flicked between the two of us. Lani kept her back turned as she dried her eyes with the back of her hands.

"We're good," I said. His eyes lingered on Lani for a beat, but she refused to face him. I cleared my throat. "Um, can you help us clear out the party, Ben? It's getting late."

He nodded. "Of course."

A while later, the clinking of bottles and rustling of discarded paper mingled with the quiet hum of cicadas outside as Lani, Benjamin, and I picked up the remnants of the party. A somber chill replaced the festive atmosphere.

As we finished up, Benjamin gathered the two garbage bags to dispose of. Once he was gone, Lani flashed me a sympathetic smile.

"I want you to have something," she said, sliding a ring off her middle finger. "Here." She took my hand and dropped the ring on my palm. It was a feathered wrap-around silver ring with a tiny silver clamp on top. It was gorgeous.

I tried the ring on, and it fit my pointer finger perfectly. "I love it, Lani."

She pressed the silver clamp and released a sharp point. "It's a self-defense ring. The blade is small, but if you aim in the right areas," she said, tapping her eye, "it'll do hell of damage."

I sighed. "Is this still about that idiot, Mark? Let's forget him already." Once I scrubbed my skin raw, I didn't want to think about him again.

"Listen," she said, gripping me by the shoulders. "The world's full of dangerous people, you know that. Promise me you will be careful?" She peered into my face seriously, voice wavering with emotion.

"Lani—"

"*Promise*," she hissed, holding out her pinkie, forcing me to pinkie swear.

"Promise."

I stepped out of the shower later and frowned, hearing raised voices. Mom and Lani were downstairs arguing. About what now? Did Lani tell her about Mark?

I tiptoed over to my room but stood in the doorway to eavesdrop.

"Really, Sloane? *I'm* selfish?" Lani demanded, her tone venomous. "I practically raised Everly while you and her dad chased after your careers. You were never there for us, but I'm the selfish one?"

I bit my lip, torn between wanting to eavesdrop and feeling guilty for doing so. The tension between Mom and Lani had always been thick, but I absolutely hated it when they went at it like this.

My dad, a deputy turned sheriff, mostly took care of us, but was often absent from home. Eventually, he packed up and moved to Wood River, two hours away from Graybury. While my mom's parents visited frequently, it was Lani who stepped up and took on the role of caretaker for me.

Lani harbored deep-seated resentment toward our mother for abandoning us for months at a time in pursuit of her law degree and admission to the Bar.

"Oh, Lani, just cut the bullshit. You can't shame me into feeling guilty for excelling in my job. Everly turned out great. I won't stand around and allow you to corrupt her, now again—why are you back in Graybury? Do you need money again?"

My ears perked up at the mention of money. Why didn't Lani come to me instead of going to Mom? I had saved close to six hundred dollars for my car.

Lani's sarcastic laughter cut through the air as I refocused on their argument. "Oh yes, you have definitely excelled," she sneered. "Playing Pick-A-Lawyer-Any-Lawyer while our broken justice system turns a blind eye to systemic racism."

"What are you talking about?"

"The murders of girls of color, right here in Graybury who are receiving little to no media attention." There was silence for a beat. Then Lani gasped. "You really don't have a clue, do you? Oh, my god. Matthias Young may have a copycat, Sloane. I'm back following leads to crack the case."

Now Mom laughed. "You solve a case? Lani, I will take

you seriously the day you finally decide to grow the hell up." Still chuckling, Mom's voice grew louder as she climbed the stairs. "Goodnight, Lani."

I retreated into the room, quietly shutting the door. My pulse raced as I sank onto the bed, processing what I'd just overheard. It sickened me the way the two people I cared about most tore each other apart with such hate. Why couldn't they just set aside their differences already? Lani and I were long past needing someone to care for us. Lani could let it go.

And Mom needed to accept that Lani was an adult now. She was free to make her own choices. None of their animosity was worth it.

After tossing restlessly with Mom's and Lani's harsh words floating around in my head, I sat up in bed. If I couldn't rest after listening to that argument, there was no way Lani could fall asleep after having the argument. I had to check on her to make sure she was okay.

I grabbed my cell phone and silently crept outside. The sky was a dark canvas, completely covered in thick, brooding clouds that blocked any glimpse of starlight. As I approached the pool house, the soft glow of a lamp illuminated the darkness. The muffled voices and soft giggles created an air of secrecy and intimacy. Peeking inside, I saw Lani and Benjamin lost in each other's embrace, their lips locked in a fiery kiss. Lani's mauve robe fell delicately around her, while Benjamin's bare chest glistened in the lamplight.

I dipped out of sight as the two broke apart. A few minutes later, their hushed voices reached the door as it slid open.

"Bye…" Lani purred. More smooching. I watched as Benjamin clumsily tugged his shirt back on and slipped away from the yard. After he got in his truck and left, Lani slid the door closed when I jumped out at her.

"Bitch," she hissed, bringing a hand to her heaving chest. She grabbed my arm and hurriedly tugged me inside the pool house, then locked the door. "What are you doing, spying on me?"

I smiled at her, at the way her eyes shone, her flustered cheeks.

She folded her arms defensively. "Why are you looking at me like that?"

"You really like him, don't you?"

She shrugged nonchalantly. "I like everybody." She sauntered into her bedroom with me trailing right behind her. I peered into her room from the doorway, at the messy bedding, the burning candles, and Lani's bikini thrown on the floor.

Oh, she liked him all right.

She glanced over her shoulder at me, observing the room, and grinned smugly. "Let's cozy up on the sofa bed. I just gotta grab my vape…" She dug around in her nightstand drawer and then straightened upon finding it. "Out, Little Miss Nosey." She playfully bumped me out of the way and pulled the door closed behind her.

"I can't help but wonder, how do you do it?" I asked out of the blue, a little while later. We were both nestled on opposite sides of the couch, snuggled under a shared blanket. Lani took a long drag from her vape as we gazed up at the ceiling.

"What are you talking about?" she replied casually.

"You know... how do you attract all these guys?" I propped myself up on one elbow to study her face.

"Sis—" She held out a hand to me. "Is this about Kyle? There will be other guys."

There *are* other guys, but they like *you*. I dropped back against my pillow, my gaze on the ceiling again. "I guess what I'm trying to say is, I don't think I'll ever have your courage."

Lani yawned. "Life's too short, Ev. You've got to take risks. You'll never get what you want if you're just sitting around waiting for things to happen. You must trust yourself. Take that first step..." Lani's words trailed off, followed by slow and even breathing.

"Lani—?" I rose on an elbow again, but she was out cold. I shifted, cozily, and stared at the ceiling again, making out faces in its bumpy texture. Lani's brazenness stuck in my mind. That heat of passion between her and Benjamin was intoxicating. I couldn't deny wanting to capture some of that flame for myself.

I glanced over at my phone laying on the coffee table, its screen beckoning me like a siren's call.

Finn.

Tucking my lip under my teeth, I reached over and grabbed my phone, Lani's words echoing in my head. Take risks.

I logged onto MatchBox and opened Finn's chat. Sure, I was treading on thin ice, but I wanted to reignite that spark between us. It was unlike anything I'd ever felt before.

A flirtatious temptress seemed to possess my thumbs as they typed out a message.

> **Lani2.0:** I can't stop thinking about you

My breaths grew warm at the sight of his three dot bubbles bouncing almost immediately.

> **Finn_D:** Yeah? Thinking what about me exactly?

Ohmigod, my mind shouted as I pressed my phone to my chest with both hands in shock. Was I truly saying these things? I closed my eyes and pictured Finn's enigmatic gaze. The hint of rugged stubble on his strong jawline. His irresistible lips...

Yes, I am definitely doing this. I returned to my phone and saw that Finn was still typing, but I was determined to up the charm even further.

My eyes narrowed. Liar. He answered my text way too quickly. His denial was kind of cute, though.

Lani2.0: Looking for a good
mystery to unravel...

I clamped a hand over my mouth to muffle my giggle.

Finn_D: Oh? Am I the
mystery?

Lani2.0: I don't know... Despite
being the stranger in town. It's your
eyes. They seem to hold secrets I'd
give anything to know

Finn_D: Anything?

I scrolled through the emoji list until I found the bikini set. Smirking, I hit SEND.

Oh. My. God. I felt as if Lani's energy had seeped into my very core, emboldening me to flirt and tease like never.

Finn_D: Lani... You're
making me blush...

I giggled again, unable to contain myself.

Hmm… I chewed on my lip thoughtfully. I really did not want to stand him up again. But what else could I do? Lani's soft snores filled the silence. Bingo.

SEVEN

I ROLLED OVER GROGGILY AND GROANED AT ALL
the noise Lani made the next morning. My left side ached,
as if I'd slept on something wrong. Bleary-eyed, I pulled
myself up to a sitting position on the couch, rubbing the
sleep from my eyes.

Lani stood in front of me, with the morning light
streaming in—casting a glow on her messy bun. She wore
white shorts with a white bralette beneath a cherry
blossom print kimono duster. The newspaper hid her face.

"What time is it?" I demanded, confused at why she was
bustling about.

Lani uttered a yelp, lowering to the floor in front of
me. "Look at this!" She jabbed a finger at a column tucked
in the top corner of the page.

"It's too early, Lani," I groaned, collapsing back onto

my pillow. My bleary eyes struggled to make out the tiny print of the article.

Finn and I really needed to stop staying up so late just to talk. But the thought of his name brought a smile to my face. Finn was an absolute sweetheart, and our chemistry was off the charts. That steamy, romantic atmosphere last night was so… yummy.

Except Finn believes he's creating all of that with Lani.

She came back into focus, chewing nervously on her nail. "…they found another body…" she uttered to herself.

"What?" I sat up again.

"Yeah—a young Latina female… Illiana Herrera…"

I leaped to my feet with newfound energy and stripped the paper from her hands. "Did you say Illiana?" I squinted at the paper, searching for her image.

"Do you know her?" Lani asked, her attention on her cell phone as she thumbed away.

My stomach twisted into a nauseating knot. I sure hoped it wasn't the woman's daughter from the diner.

BODY IDENTIFIED AS NINETEEN-YEAR-OLD, ILLIANA HERRERA the headline read. There wasn't a photo, but the details were horrid.

I slowly sat back on the couch, wanting more than anything not to have that information in my head—the thought of Illiana's lifeless body... her fingers...

"Sick," I whispered.

Lani glanced up from her phone, gasping heavily. "Oh shit, Sloane's on TV!" She lunged for the remote on the coffee table and clicked on the screen. She flicked through the stations, and there Mom was, at a news conference that was already underway.

A hand flew over my mouth. Mom stood behind the podium clutching an 8x10 picture of Illiana—identical to the one her mother had in the diner. It was her.

"Let me be clear," Mom said, her voice firm. "I find the media's apathetic response to this case unsettling. They plaster white victims' faces on every screen and newspaper..." She paused, her icy blue eyes scanning the room to ensure she had everyone's full attention.

Lani lowered onto the couch beside me, whistling softly. "Well, she finally went there," she said, a hint of admiration in her voice.

I felt the tension radiating from the screen as Mom continued. She raised Illiana's image for everyone to see.

"Illiana Herrera matters, and she deserves justice—as do all victims of color. We cannot continue to let bias dictate which lives we deem worthy of our attention and concern."

The reporters erupted into a frenzy of questions, their voices overlapping. But one query rose above the rest.

"Isn't this crime similar to the ones committed by Matthias Young, the Graybury Slayer?"

Mom's steely gaze never faltered. "We are scrutinizing all potential connections. Given Young's recent passing, it is possible that we are dealing with a copycat killer. We won't rest until we uncover the truth and bring whoever is responsible to justice."

The sounds of clattering dishes and sizzling food did little to quell the turmoil in my mind. Even days later, working in the diner, the news of Illiana's murder still weighed heavily on me. Though I never knew her, the desperation in her mother's gaze that day haunted me relentlessly.

The serial killer was all Graybury could talk about since Mom's news conference. Already they'd given him a name—the Trophy Killer. Customers whispered about him in hushed tones, their gossip spreading through the diner like a virus.

The bell on the diner door jingled as another customer walked in. I kept my eyes down, focusing on the glass I was wiping clean behind the counter. I didn't want to make eye contact or get drawn into another hushed conversation.

"Coffee, ma'am?" I asked the woman who'd just sat at the counter, avoiding her gaze. I topped off her mug, my hands shivering.

Mom would find out who did this. If she could take down the Graybury Slayer that many years ago, she could get justice for Illiana and the others.

Lately, Mom had been practicing in other areas of the law. Recently, she had been expanding her legal practice beyond the usual scope. As the sole attorney in Graybury, she dealt with a range of cases including residential leasing, probate court filings, and tax appeals. Mom was practically Graybury's hero. If she was a part of Illiana's case, there was hope for justice. I clung to that, willing my nerves to settle.

"Order's up," the cook called. I wondered if he ever got sick of saying that.

I collected the two plates of smoldering hot food and approached table five, where two middle-aged men sat discussing the Trophy Killer, of course. One of them glanced up at me, his eyes flicking to my nametag before he spoke.

"Everly, huh? You're that attorney's daughter?"

I nodded, swallowing hard. "Yeah."

"Must be tough, having to work on another case like this," he said, sympathy coloring his voice.

"Uh-huh," I agreed, setting their meals on the table, my hands trembling again. "She's doing her best, though."

"Of course, of course," the man said. "You tell her we're all rooting for her, okay?"

"Will do," I replied, forcing a grateful smile. As I walked away, I couldn't help but feel a strange mix of pride and apprehension. My mom was the town's hope for justice, and I knew she wouldn't let them down. But at what cost? The pressure was immense, and I could only imagine how it weighed on her.

I took a deep breath and forced myself to focus on the task at hand—serving customers, clearing tables, and trying not to let my thoughts drift back to Illiana's horrifying death.

I balanced a tray of dirty dishes on my hip, taking in how crowded and noisy the diner was for a Tuesday. Just then, Finn walked in right behind a trio of teenagers, his stormy eyes scanning the diner for an empty seat. My body

tensed as his gaze eventually fixed on to the stool right
next to me. I hadn't laid eyes on him since spying on him
at the pastry shop.

Shifting the tray of dirty dishes, I braced myself for a
greeting, but Finn sat without looking twice at me. He
was completely unaware of the secret connection between
us—of all the things I knew about him that he didn't
know I did. Even though I wanted nothing more than for
him to turn around and realize it was me there, a part of
me also liked that invisible bond between us.

I slowly turned away, mentally grinning. It was a thrill
having a secret connection that he was completely
oblivious to.

I put away the dirty dishes and grabbed a fresh pot of
coffee to offer to Finn. I knew he loved his coffee black.
Eager to sneak another glance at Finn, I hurried into the
dining area and almost shattered the coffee pot into a
million pieces.

Lani stood in line at the grab and go counter, literally
three seats over from Finn.

My heart leaped into my throat. What was Lani doing
here? I watched her intently as she had a heated
conversation on her cell.

"Look, I'm telling you, this information is crucial," she
snapped into her phone, her voice loud enough to turn

heads. My eyes darted back and forth between her and Finn. "No—*no*…" Lani's voice climbed. "Do you realize how much of my time you've wasted?"

I took a wobbly step back as Finn glanced over and laid eyes on Lani. His eyes lit up as he placed both hands on the counter, beginning to rise.

Ohmigod. Ohmigod, I silently repeated. My secret was about to unravel and there was nothing I could do except watch things spiral out of control. A bead of sweat trickled down the side of my face as Finn stood, his eyes locked on Lani. His lips turned up into a smile I'd never seen on his face before.

My heart hammered against my ribcage, threatening to burst out of my chest. The diner's buzz seemed to fade into the background, leaving only the sound of my own ragged breaths.

Finn strode toward Lani with a determined expression, while she remained completely unaware, still engrossed in her phone call. I could almost see the gears turning in his head as he reached her side.

I told him Lani was going back to college. And yet there she was.

"Hey—what a surprise," Finn cried, beaming at Lani as if she were a celebrity.

Lani's eyes flicked up to meet his, but she only offered

him a polite smile and returned to her phone call. "No. You promised me you'd… Fine. I'll meet you in five minutes." She hung up on her call, sighing heavily.

I dashed into the kitchen before she could spot me, but I continued to watch the scene unfold through the squared windowpanes on the double doors. Finn spoke to Lani again, but I couldn't make out what he was saying because the dishwasher roared monstrously behind me. I wanted to turn and scream at it, but I couldn't peel my eyes away from Finn and Lani.

Lani shook her head in disagreement about whatever Finn said, barely even acknowledging him. But Finn was persistent, his hands gesturing excitedly.

Come on, Finn, just let it go already. I knew how Lani reacted to unwanted attention. She lost it.

But Finn wasn't letting up. I saw the frustration mounting in his gray-blue eyes, realizing something was terribly wrong.

My hand flew over my mouth as Finn reached inside his pocket and pulled out his phone.

He was going to show her the MatchBox profile.

My brain chanted, "no, no, no!" as fear paralyzed my body. I couldn't believe I'd done something so careless and stupid.

Someone brushed by me and went out the kitchen

doors, and as they did, Lani's raised voice wavered inside.

"I'm sorry, but I already said I *don't* know you," she snapped. She hastily grabbed her pastry and coffee before storming off to meet whoever had upset her on the phone.

Finn flinched as if she had spat in his face. The pain and shame were evident on his face as he watched Lani leave. Confusion clouded his eyes as he searched for any witnesses to his public humiliation.

I quickly lowered out of sight. The cat was so out of the bag. I squeezed my eyes shut, wishing I had the guts to go out there and explain myself, but I just couldn't.

"Everly, what are you doing down there? Get out of the way," Paisley hissed.

"I'm looking for something," I lied, feeling along the floor as she stepped around me. My phone pinged in my pocket. I slowly stood and peeked out the window. Finn sat at the counter with his head bent down, staring at his phone.

I lowered to the floor again, a trillion percent certain he was the one texting me. I nibbled on my lip, shakily retrieving my cell. It was a MatchBox notification.

My vision blurred with tears, reading Finn's quick message.

> **Finn_D:** What sort of sick and twisted game are you playing?

Tears blurred my vision as I stared at the phone, Finn's furious message illuminating the screen. This wasn't how it was supposed to happen. They were never supposed to cross paths. Why didn't I step in or try to stop it? Instead, I hid in the kitchen like a coward.

Either way, the charade needed to end. I couldn't keep playing this game any longer. Finn deserved an explanation. An apology. Yet, my thumb hovered over the keyboard, unable to type a response. Shame engulfed me, leaving me paralyzed.

After hastily wiping my eyes, I glanced out the window, but Finn had disappeared. With a heavy heart, I closed MatchBox without a clue about what to do next. It hadn't even crossed my mind that Finn and Lani might run into each other in this tiny town—it was practically impossible for them not to.

Panic set in as I realized how screwed I was. My phone buzzed once again, another MatchBox notification from Finn.

Fear quickly overcame my hurt feelings. What did Finn's statement mean? What was he planning without knowing my identity? Or had he somehow already discovered the truth? He couldn't have. I was practically invisible to him.

Finn was understandably upset. If the situation were reversed, I couldn't imagine how I would feel.

How could I have put someone in this position?

———

When I got home that evening, I reflexively checked my phone for any updates from Finn. But there was nothing. In a moment of desperation, I scrolled through my contacts and found Lani's name. She deserved to know the truth about my foolish actions. Maybe she could help fix things or even reach out to Finn on my behalf. Perhaps they could even bond over my idiocy.

Without hesitation, I composed and sent the message to Lani.

> Can we talk later? I have something to tell you

Lani replied instantly, probably because she was already thumbing away on her phone.

> Of course, sis. See you 2nite @ 10

EIGHT

the next morning. Still no answer from Lani. She was not
home when I got back last night, and she didn't meet me
at ten o'clock as she'd planned. I waited for hours, but she
never came.

I scrolled through the notifications on my phone,
breath catching, when I saw Finn's name. But there
weren't any new messages from him. His angry texting
had stopped abruptly, leaving me unsure how to feel.
Should I be relieved, or should I freak out? The latter
seemed unfair, considering I'd played with his heart.

With a frustrated huff, I dropped the phone on the bed.
A creepy feeling crawled up my spine, causing
goosebumps to rise on my skin. I couldn't pinpoint why.

Who was I kidding? It was the guilt gnawing away at

me. Admitting to catfishing someone with Lani's identity was going to have serious consequences. Lani was going to kill me for it, for sure.

Groaning, I rolled over and forced myself out of bed. The sooner I got this off my chest, the better. I washed up and got dressed, pulling on a pair of khaki shorts and a navy-blue dolman sleeve tee, and rushed to the staircase. But my pace slowed as I approached the kitchen where Mom and Gus sat.

"Morning, Everly. Gus brought bagels," Mom said, shifting to sit in her seat properly. She'd had one leg across Gus's lap as they skimmed over her tablet. Gus was a lawyer, too.

"Have you seen Lani today?" I asked, totally ignoring him and the fresh bouquet in the center of the table.

Mom smoothed a hand through her hair, forcing a thin smile at my rudeness. "Not this morning."

"She's probably sleeping in," Gus offered, as if anyone asked him. But that sort of made sense.

With purposeful steps, I marched toward the back door, determined to check the pool house. As my hand reached for the metal knob, Mom's voice stopped me in my tracks.

"Your dad called," she said, her tone casual as she calmly popped a piece of bagel into her mouth. "He's going to be in town this weekend and hopes you two can catch up."

My breath caught in my throat at the mention of Dad. It had been months, maybe even a year, since we last spoke face to face. After he became sheriff and moved away, our communication reduced to occasional phone calls that often went unanswered.

I tried to play it cool as I shrugged my shoulders nonchalantly. "K." My voice sounded insignificant compared to the weight of emotions stirring inside of me. But I will think about him later. Right now, I needed to find Lani.

"Hey, Ev," I heard Benjamin call once I'd gotten outside.

I spun around, squinting, spotting him kneeling among the vibrant flowerbeds, pruning shears in hand. I couldn't help recalling the passionate encounter between him and Lani where Benjamin had Lani pressed against the wall, their tongues in each other's mouths.

My cheeks flushed at the memory. I still couldn't believe prim and proper Benjamin had it in him. Clearing my throat awkwardly, I waved, nibbling on my lip. No use beating around the bush. "Have you seen Lani this morning?"

Benjamin's expression remained impassive. "I'm afraid

not." He wiped his brow with the back of his hand, leaving a streak of dirt. "You look... antsy... Everything okay?"

My gaze drifted to the pool house, uncertainty gripping me. "I don't know. She's not answering my texts."

"Maybe her phone's charging," he suggested.

"Maybe..." But I was skeptical. Lani could still use her phone if it was being charged. Something about her absence felt... off.

I hesitantly approached the glass door, half-hoping to find Lani lounging on the couch, but it sat vacant. Where was she?

"Lani?" I gently knocked, unsure if I really wanted to disturb her if she was sleeping. No answer. My knuckles rapped against the door again, this time with more force.

Nothing.

Sighing, I gripped the door handle and paused, torn between respecting Lani's privacy and my anxiety. But why hadn't she answered my calls all night? Was she that busy, or did she just not want to talk to me?

My heart sank. What if she found out about MatchBox already? I had to talk to her and explain myself.

Pushing my glasses off my nose, I cautiously entered the pool house. Despite my growing sense of unease, I tried to convince myself that I was just overreacting, as usual. Lani couldn't possibly be mad at me because of MatchBox. She was probably in her bedroom, nursing a hangover and hiding from the world behind closed curtains. Maybe she even had a fling over.

"Lani?" I tapped on her bedroom door. I creaked open the door just to peek, expecting to find her in bed, but a startled gasp escaped my throat as I pushed the door wider. Lani's room was the same way it'd been a couple nights ago, after sleeping with Benjamin—sheets tossed haphazardly, blown-out candles on the nightstand, her swimsuit abandoned on the floor, untouched. The only difference was the closet door was slightly ajar from her change of clothes yesterday. Did this mean Lani just didn't come home at all? Or was she…in danger?

Immediately, I tried calling her again, certain something must've been wrong. It went straight to voicemail, as it had all night when I attempted to reach her. Anxiety clawed at my chest at the thought of the Trophy Killer, and Lani's determination to track him. Suddenly, the air inside the pool house felt heavy and suffocating, causing me to stumble through the sliding door outside, gasping for breath.

I ran back to the house, knowing I had to get Mom.

"Everly, what happened?" Benjamin asked while starting to his feet out of the corner of my eye.

"I—I'm not sure," I answered breathlessly, bursting through the backdoor. Mom and Gus's soft chuckles fueled my growing agitation as I stood there, struggling to catch my breath. How could they be so carefree and oblivious?

"Lani didn't come home last night," I blurted out.

Mom glanced up, reading my expression. "Everly, I'm sure Lani's fine. You know how your sister can be," she said dismissively, taking a sip of her coffee.

"But she's not returning my calls or my texts. Her phone is going straight to voicemail."

"She could be over at a friend's house," Gus said, that cheesy smile on his face as he threw out one absurd possibility after another, each suggestion more infuriating than the last. "Or maybe she's gone jogging and lost cell connection. Or maybe she could've met a guy…" His eyes flicked to mine as if we shared some secret joke. "Or…"

"Maybe you don't know my sister the way I do," I snapped, the pulsating ache behind my eyes intensifying. "Lani planned to meet me at ten last night because I had something important to say. She wouldn't have bailed on me." I took a shaky breath, forcing my tears to stay at bay. "I think we need to file a missing person's report."

"*Everly*," Mom clipped. "You need to calm down," she said, exchanging a worried glance with Gus.

"You're overreacting to nothing. I know Lani as well, and she's unreliable. She's most likely lost in her own carelessness. Just have some patience—she'll eventually show up."

"Fine." I spun on my heel and stormed out of the kitchen, hot tears blurring my vision and anger boiling in my chest.

The wheels of my bike spun frantically as I raced to the sheriff's barely ten minutes later. Every passing minute felt like an eternity as thoughts of Illiana Herrera's lifeless body filled my mind, reminding me I failed to report her as a missing person. But this time, it was different. This time, it was Lani in danger, and I refused to make the same mistake twice. The police needed to look for her. Now. If I was wrong, and Lani reappeared—then great. Better to be safe than sorry.

I approached the sheriff's office, its darkened windows offering no comfort or solace. Steeling myself for the inevitable confrontation, I pulled open the heavy door and stepped into the dimly lit room.

"Excuse me," I said, voice trembling slightly. I cleared my throat and straightened my spine. "I need to file a missing person's report."

The fluorescent lights flickered overhead, casting a sickly pallor on the deputy's face as he stood behind the reception desk. He looked up from his paperwork, his eyes serious.

I stepped up to the desk, trying to keep my nerves in check. Although I hoped filing the report was the right decision, I hoped even more that this was a false alarm.

I studied the deputy's face. He couldn't have been much older than me. His frame was scrawny beneath his khaki suit, which accompanied his light brown skin. He had thick coiled hair, and big puppy dog eyes behind a pair of round glasses. He practically screamed amateur. How was he going to find my sister?

"Okay," he said, shuffling around on the desk, searching for a report sheet. He clumsily knocked over a cup of pens. Sneaking me a glance, he pushed his glasses off his nose nervously. Finally, he found the paper.

And I started rambling. "My sister is missing. She didn't come home last night, even though she promised to meet me at ten o'clock. She's not answering my texts. Her phone is going straight to voicemail…"

He nodded, listening intently to my every word. "Is your sister over eighteen?"

"Yes. Why?"

"I—" he began, rubbing the back of his neck. "I understand your concern, but for individuals over the age of eighteen, we must wait seventy-two hours before filing a missing persons report."

Anger flared in me as I blinked at him. "You're telling me I'm supposed to just ignore something terrible could be happening to my sister at this very moment…?" I glanced at his badge. "Deputy Fuller? You're Deputy A-Hole?" The words slipped from my lips.

"I don't understand…"

"I called you and tried to report Illiana Herrera missing. You accused me of making a prank call and now look at what's happened." My voice broke. Tears wet my face.

His eyes widened momentarily before composing himself. He shuffled around behind the desk and offered me a tissue that I reluctantly accepted. "You have every right to be upset at that," he said. "I sincerely apologize. We'd received multiple prank calls all week, and I assumed… Well, that's not important. You were right, and I should've listened. My apologies."

I dried my face and took a deep breath. "What about my sister?"

"We can fill out this form in advance, and after seventy-two hours, still with no word from your sister, we will do everything we can to find her."

The thought of just letting the minutes tick left me with a heavy heart. But what other choice did I have? Maybe that's why Mom wasn't in such a hurry to do anything. She already knew the protocol.

Sighing, I rattled off Lani's details, each word feeling like a stone dropping into the pit of my stomach. As he scribbled down the information, I glared at him, wondering if he truly cared, or if he was just going through the motions.

When he finished, he locked eyes with me, his eyes reflecting a quiet sadness. "I really am sorry about before," he said, as if reading my mind. "I know waiting is going to be unbearable but…" He paused, pulling a small notepad from his pocket, and scribbled something down. He tore off the sheet of paper and handed it to me. "This is my direct line. If anything changes before then, or if you just need someone to talk to, call me."

I took the paper and swiftly read over the numbers. He'd written his first name—Chance. "Thank you, Chance. I'm Everly, by the way."

He nodded curtly. "Nice to meet you." And with that, I left the station, tucking his number into my pocket.

Outside, the sky was heavy with clouds threatening rain, and something just told me that was a bad sign.

NINE

THE RAIN PATTERED AGAINST THE DINER'S window later, blurring the streetlights outside into a hazy glow, the empty diner echoing with dread. But then the bell chimed, and the door swung open.

My breath caught. But it was only Mrs. Chen collecting her to-go order. I handed her the bag, forcing a smile to mask the turmoil brewing inside me. Each customer that walked through the door today made my heart race, hoping it would be Lani, safe and sound, ready to explain everything. But she never came.

My phone sat face-up next to the register, as I willed it to light up with Lani's name. I kept replaying in my head what I remembered about that heated conversation she had on the phone. Who was she talking to so passionately? Did they know about her sudden disappearance?

As the door shut behind Mrs. Chen, the diner fell silent

again. There hadn't been much traffic—probably because of the rain. Or perhaps the Trophy Killer kept everyone at bay.

I gazed out the window at the rain pouring down in sheets. Lani was out there in that storm somewhere. I hoped she was at least some place safe, warm, and dry.

A shiver went up my spine. Despite the heavy downpour, Lou still had the A/C cranked too high.

My phone lit up with a notification and I pounced on it. But it was only spam. I sank back, nerves electrified.

Sighing, I glanced at the second hand on the clock ticking mercilessly. My desperation was turning into anger as every minute passed. I wanted answers, and I wanted them now. But I had to wait three whole days before I could officially report Lani as missing.

I blinked rapidly, my eyes stinging with tears. My sister was *missing*.

Mom wanted to dismiss it with her usual tough love tactics. And she was right. Lani was the daring one, the wild child who flirted with danger and pushed boundaries, but this was different. Lani agreed to meet up last night. There was no chance she would leave without telling me. Something or someone was preventing her from using her phone.

A sickening bomb exploded in my stomach at that

revelation. I clamped my hand over my mouth, forcing my insides to settle.

I needed to remind myself that this was Lani. And I knew without a doubt that whatever was happening, Lani would put up a fight. She was capable of anything with her quick wit and grounded thinking.

Biting my cheek, tears threatened to spill over. This was a torturous experience.

Grabbing my phone, I dialed Lani's number. After the beep, I took a shaky breath and left her a desperate voice message.

"Hey, um—as you can see, I'm really worried about you. Will you please call me back as soon as possible? Love you."

As I carefully set the cell phone down on the counter, it suddenly vibrated. My hand snatched it up in an instant, hoping to see a message from Lani. But it was a MatchBox notification, except this one wasn't from Finn. My eyes fixated on the username: 10462, its profile picture nothing but a stark black square. But it was the contents of the message that gave me pause.

> **10462:** Nice try pretending to be Lani

I licked my dry lips, my breaths shallow.

Lani2.0: Who is this?

The reply was almost instantaneous.

10462: Who are YOU?

I rolled my eyes. Finn. I understood he was upset, but Lani was missing. I couldn't really deal with him right now.

Lani2.0: Finn... I'm sorry, okay? I won't ever bother you again

I slammed my phone down, my stomach twisting into knots. What did he hope to gain out of texting me from another account?

Giving me a dose of my own medicine, I reminded myself, stupidly pushing my glasses off my nose. I would eventually tell him the truth once Lani came back. Now just wasn't the time.

My phone lit up with another text.

10462: I'm not Finn

My insides turned cold, and I stared at the phone, unable to move or breathe. Was Finn just toying with me?

Or could this really be someone else? Who else would know that I was pretending to be Lani? And where was Lani?

Lou stepped out of the kitchen. "Mrs. Chen was our last takeout order," he said, circling around me and taking a double look. "Are you feeling okay?"

I bit my lip, struggling to gather my composure. "Sure—just a headache…" I lied, although I felt one coming on.

Lou shook his head. "Those are the worst. You can take off, kid. I'll call you a cab."

"You sure?"

He gestured to the downpour outside. "I don't see much more business coming in tonight. Go home and get some rest. And stay safe out there."

Rain drummed against the cab's roof several minutes later. It was relentless, a torrential downpour—almost as if the universe mourned Lani's disappearance right along with me.

I quickly dialed Lani's number, my fingers shaking in desperation. I knew I would just get her voicemail for the umpteenth time, but I couldn't help holding onto a glimmer of hope that she might pick up. She never did.

Everything was falling apart. Finn knew I catfished him. Lani was missing, and now someone else knew about my impersonation of her. It was all too much to process at once. But I couldn't let myself dwell on the chaos. Finding my sister was all that mattered.

Maybe she had returned to campus? I made a mental note to comb the pool house and call her roommates if I didn't find anything.

A small sense of relief washed over me as I allowed myself to relax slightly, but the weight of the situation still hung heavily on my shoulders.

When I reached the house, its familiar façade was barely visible through the curtain of rain. As I got up the stoop and fumbled with my keys, the front door suddenly flew open. It was Mom—flustered with wide eyes. She looked like a woman on the edge of a precipice, forced to take a leap into the unknown.

"Mom?" I took a step back, surprised.

Her car keys were in one hand, her other hand up to her ear, clutching her phone. "I have to get to the station right away," she called over her shoulder, already rushing to her car.

"Wait—is it about Lani?" I asked urgently, my heart sinking into my stomach.

Mom paused, her face lined with worry. "Just stay put until I get back. And lock the door," she added. Then she peeled out of the driveway, leaving me standing in the rain.

Something was very wrong. I'd never seen Mom's eyes look like that before—so panicked.

As I watched the taillights disappear into the rain-soaked night, a cold dread settled over me. For the first time, I truly understood the meaning of fear.

———

I cautiously slid open the door to the pool house, my heart racing with anticipation. Inside, everything appeared just as it had earlier when I peeked in. But this time, I meticulously searched every nook and cranny, checking under the bed, rummaging through drawers, and even looking in Lani's closet. I found her clothes still unpacked, and her vape returned to its rightful place in the nightstand drawer.

It was impossible for Lani to go back to campus and leave all this behind. The thought was too absurd.

As I made my way toward the exit, I couldn't help but survey the eerily silent pool house one last time. My eyes landed on Lani's messenger bag hanging on a coat hook. A sharp gasp escaped my throat at the sight. There was no way she would have forgotten something so important. Without thinking, I grabbed the bag and brought it back to my room.

I stood in the doorway, rain dripping from my hair and clothes, feeling more alone than ever. My hands trembled as I dabbed at my pooling eyes. I paced back and forth, trying to ignore the sickening knot in my stomach.

Lani wouldn't have left without her things. Something was wrong.

What was Mom not telling me? She needed to get to the station. Why? Was it to do with Lani or the Trophy Killer? Or both? My pacing slowed as I remembered Chance. He could tell me what was happening down there.

I shook with anticipation while dialing his number. But his phone rang and rang. Did I not dial the correct number? Retracting my hand, I studied the numbers once more. Frustration coursed through me as I yearned for answers. Despite pressing CALL again and again, Chance refused to answer. I was so irritated I could punch something.

But wait—if they needed Mom at the station, clearly something major was going down. Something that would require all law enforcement to be present. Chance must've been too busy to have his phone.

I exhaled. While I knew I should respect that, I still needed to know if there was a development on Lani. So, I selfishly dialed Chance again, and that time, he answered.

"Hello?" His voice was low and hushed.

"Chance? It's Everly. My mom… What's going on?" I demanded, cutting to the chase.

"Everly—"

"Chance, I need to know if all this chaos is about my sister. Is it Lani?" His hesitation made my blood run cold. "Did they find her?"

"No. But…"

"But what?"

"We found a broken cell phone we believe is hers."

A broken cell phone? What did that mean? That Lani lost her phone? Okay, so, clearly that's why my calls weren't going through. But did that mean she was in trouble?

"Were there signs of a struggle?" I said, blurting out my thoughts.

"Everly, I shouldn't be telling you any of this. I've already said too much," he said, his voice lowered.

Again, with stupid protocols. I tried to report my sister missing hours ago. Had they acted then and searched for her, none of this would have unfolded.

"Yes, or no?" I spat into the phone.

Chance uttered a wet sound before replying. "Yes."

———

I hopped on my bike and rushed into the night, the darkness swallowing me whole. I was like a moth drawn to flame, desperate for answers. Where did they find Lani's phone? What sort of struggles were there? Where was Lani now?

The chilly rain stung my face as I pedaled furiously through the small-town streets, each streetlight casting eerie shadows on the wet pavement. My heart pounded in time with the rhythm of my bike, echoing my growing fear.

When the sheriff's station finally came into view, I skidded to a stop, breathless and soaked to the bone. I was here now. There was no turning back.

My bike hit the pavement as I leaped off and dashed into the building, my wet shoes squeaking on the linoleum. The scent of stale coffee and damp paper filled my nostrils, bringing a strange sense of familiarity to this foreign nightmare.

I scanned the area, searching for any sign of my mother or Lani. But only the secretary sat at the desk. She jumped at my abrupt entrance.

"How can I help you?" she asked.

Can you help me find my sister is what I wanted to ask. "I'm Sloane Baker's daughter, Everly. Is my mom here?" I wrapped my arms around myself, shivering from the wetness, cold and nerves.

"Everly?" Chance appeared and squeaked at me. After glancing over his shoulder, he hurried over. "You're not supposed to be here," he whispered. He checked over his shoulder again. "You didn't mention your mother was Sloane Baker," he hissed, grabbing my arm and leading me to the door. "She will kill me if she knows I told you anything."

I was so done listening to his warnings about protocols. "Chance, I don't care about any of that. Just tell me if my sister is okay. What type of struggle did you...?"

His walkie talkie crackled, and a voice came across. "*We have located the victim's car... abandoned on Heather Lane...*"

Chance and I locked eyes. He reached out and caught me just as my knees buckled. Victim? Abandoned car? What was happening?

At that moment, all sense of rational thinking flew out the window. Panic set into every cell in my body. My heart felt like it was about to leap out of my chest as I gasped for air. "I can't breathe," I whispered.

"Go home," Chance insisted.

I stumbled backward, but Chance caught hold of me again. "Really… I can't…" My words choked and my vision blurred.

"Hey—look at me." He placed both hands on my shoulder, coaxing me to breathe. "Inhale through your nose… Hold it." He counted to four under his breath. "Now exhale slowly for four." He counted softly again, gently squeezing my shoulders. We repeated that a couple more times until Mom's sharp tone broke my focus.

"Everly—?"

Chance let go of me and backed away quickly.

"What's she doing here?" Mom yelled at him. "Did you call her? What are you telling her?"

"Mom, no." I shook my head, struggling to gather my words. I briefly repeated Chance's breathing exercise before swallowing hard and facing Mom. "I came here to find out what's going on. What are the developments on Lani?"

"Everly, go home and wait until I call you later," she said, eying me with the same piercing intensity she used to dismantle criminals in her courtroom. Only I wasn't one of her perps. That tactic couldn't work on me. I had the right to know what was happening with my sister.

With my shoulders squared and an unyielding gaze, I stated firmly, "I will not be leaving, Mom. Lani's my sister and I deserve to be here and know what's happening, too."

Her mouth opened, and then her phone rang. She listened to her caller for a beat, but then she held the phone away to give Chance the evil eye. "Put her in the interview room. And get her out of those wet clothes," she added before turning away, bringing the phone back to her ear. "I don't care about the goddamn rain," she hissed into the phone as she marched away.

When Mom was gone, Chance pushed his glasses off his nose, shifting nervously, avoiding my eyes. "Um, if you want to follow me…" He took an awkward step forward.

I had to hurry to keep up with him as he took quick strides, almost as if he wanted to get away from me. But I understood it. I'd gotten him into trouble—which was far from my intentions. All I wanted was to find Lani. And I would move heaven and earth to do that if needed.

We reached a hallway with several doors on either side, each labeled with a number. He opened the number 7 door and stepped back to let me enter first. It was a small room, just big enough for two chairs and one table. A single fluorescent lamp hung from the ceiling, providing the only source of illumination in the room. A shiver went up my spine at its cold yet sterile environment. Chance said nothing as he directed me to sit in the chair.

I slinked to a seat, nervously glancing at the mirror that

lined one wall, wondering if someone stood behind it, watching me.

Chance shuffled from foot to foot as if he didn't know what to do with himself. Then, after several seconds, he finally spoke. "I'll be back with something dry for you to wear. Just wait here." He slipped out and shut the door behind him.

I settled into the hard seat and folded my arms, hoping to warm up. But water trickled down my back from my damp hair and my entire body trembled.

After what felt like hours, Chance returned with a bundle of folded dark clothes and a fleece blanket. He extended the items to me, still not quite meeting my eyes.

Sighing, I accepted the clothes. He silently left, leaving me to get changed. I eyed the mirror wearily, still unsure who or what was back there. There was no way I was about to undress in front of them. I pulled the oversized sweatpants over my damp shorts and slipped into the sweatshirt that was so large it practically swallowed me whole. The sleeves came down to my knuckles. But even in dry clothes, I still couldn't shake my chill. So, I wrapped the scratchy blanket around my shoulders as I took my seat again. Immediately, Chance came back inside, this time clutching a paper coffee cup with a lid. He slid the cup across the table to me.

I stared at it and then at him. "I don't drink coffee."

"Me either," he said, finally looking me in the eye. "And it's not coffee, but tea—chamomile—to help you relax. You were hyperventilating back there, so I thought…" He shrugged, rubbing the back of his neck shyly.

I straightened, my gaze softening. I wanted to calm down. Lani's disappearance put my nerves on edge. I was exhausted. "Thank you," I croaked, wrapping my fingers around the warm cup, inhaling the sweet honey. "Are you going to sit—or…?"

"I'm not telling you any more information," he said, fidgeting with the back of the chair across from me.

My heart sank as I realized how futile this conversation was likely to be. I had a sip of tea, trying to mask my disappointment and anger. It didn't matter, though. I felt better now that I was inside the station. I wasn't leaving until I heard something—anything that might lead me closer to finding Lani. Someone would have to tell me something.

My gaze met his. "I'm sorry if I got you into any trouble back there." I nodded behind him.

He bit his lip thoughtfully before slowly lowering into the chair. "It's all right. Being the rookie, I always take the most heat around here. Even if things aren't my fault, people just like to blame me for it."

I slid my fingers up and down the cup, trying to warm my fingertips. "Why stay here then?"

His mouth parted slightly, totally surprised by the question. But then he pressed his lips together without a word. We sat in silence as I finished my tea. I don't know when or how, but I fell asleep, bundled in oversized clothes and the scratchy blanket, head resting in my folded arms on the table.

Then a ferocious animal wail tore through the station. It was my mom.

TEN

I WOKE UP WITH A START AND FRANTICALLY looked around, unsure how long I'd been asleep. Chance was nowhere to be seen. Mom's screams bounced off the walls, piercing my ears and jolted me into action. With trembling hands, I slid back in my seat, knocking over my cup and spilled a few droplets of tea on the table.

"Mom!" I shrieked, fear gripping my chest. The agony in her voice was unmistakable. I threw open the door and sprinted down the narrow hallway, my glasses sliding down the bridge of my nose. Panic consumed me, my breaths coming out in short, painful gasps. As I turned the corner, I spotted them—my mom on the floor, her face streaked with tears. Chance was there, trying to comfort her, while another deputy stood guard over them.

A sinking feeling settled in my stomach. I burst into wretched sobs, finally getting the answer I'd been seeking all day. Lani was gone.

Mom didn't have to say the words. I could see it written across her face, hear it in every ragged breath. Lani was dead.

"Where is she?" I choked out. Chance glanced up, finally noticing my presence, and approached me solemnly.

"I'm sorry, Everly," he whispered.

"Where is my sister?"

"Everly—" Chance shook his head, his own anguish plain on his face. "Trust me, you don't want to see Lani like that."

My hand flew over my mouth as I stumbled against the wall and slid to the floor. "What did they do to her?" I wailed.

Chance lowered in front of me. He gripped my shoulders, attempting to console me. My eyes darted from Chance to Mom, who was still on the floor, her sobs echoing through the hallway. Her pain was palpable, a living thing that clawed at my chest and demanded attention. I hesitated for a moment before breaking away from Chance's embrace and crawling toward her.

Mom was on all fours, wailing into the linoleum floor.

My heart shattered into a million pieces at the sight of her. She looked at me with bloodshot eyes as her trembling hands reached for me. "Ev…" she squeaked, clinging to me as though I were her lifeline.

We sobbed in each other's arms.

"Goddamn it…" Sherriff Abernathy's voice rang out. "Deputies, please escort these two into an interview room now."

Chance and the other deputy moved swiftly to separate us, Chance hooking an arm under me to help me to my feet. His wide eyes were full of pain behind his glasses.

"I'm sorry, Everly," he said again, voice laced with sorrow.

I wanted to slap the words right out of his mouth. Sorry wouldn't bring Lani back. Sorry wouldn't make this nightmare go away.

I allowed Chance to lead me back into the interrogation room—only this time, Mom sat beside me. She held her face in her hands as Sheriff Abernathy stood across from us.

He was a tall, thin man in his late fifties with a weathered face that spoke of years under the sun. He tapped his ivory fingers on the table nervously, unsure where to start. Finally, he cleared his throat. "We have to talk about when you last saw Lani… What did she…?"

"We know who did this already, Abernathy," Mom uttered through clenched teeth, glaring at him with bitter hatred. She rubbed her temples, leaving red marks on her skin.

"Sloane—" the sheriff started, but Mom cut him off with a sharp glare.

"We know damn well this is the Trophy Killer. He targeted Lani because of my press conference."

Sheriff Abernathy nodded. "I—agree with you entirely. Which is why," he interjected, his voice heavy with authority, "I have to remove you from this case, Sloane. With your personal connection and potential conflict of interest…"

"Are you serious?" I interrupted, unable to believe my ears. Someone murdered our loved one, and he's concerned about some bureaucratic rule? I spun to Mom—waiting for her to give him a piece of her mind. But she sat there stone-faced and compliant. *"Mom?"* I shook her shoulder, trying to snap her out of it.

Her tired, haunted eyes resembled a woman in some noir thriller as she blinked at me and sided with him. "He's right, Ev. It's the law." She glanced at the sheriff, a fleeting flash of anger crossing her features. "I'm trusting you will catch this twisted bastard, Abernathy."

"You have my word, Sloane," he said earnestly, only I

didn't believe him.

How many victims had already fallen prey to the Trophy Killer?

I gasped. My neck snapped up as I stared at them both. "What proof says the Trophy Killer is responsible?" I demanded, heart slinking to my toes. "Did he…take something from Lani?"

Mom sighed, covering her face with her hands. "Dear god," she uttered under her breath.

"Mom, please!" I clutched her arm and begged.

She shifted my way, her eyes glassy and far away. Her lips trembled as she struggled to speak. "He—he shaved Lani's head. They didn't find a single strand of her hair."

My mouth opened, but I couldn't speak. A tear rolled down my cheek. Imagining Lani's lifeless form lying there, her once-vibrant hair cruelly snipped away, sent a wave of nausea through me. It was all too much.

"I told you something was wrong." My voice was barely a whisper, choked by guilt and regret.

Mom's eyes flashed as she spun to me sharply. "We are not playing the blame game. No one is responsible except for that sick and twisted bastard out there preying on innocent girls." Even as she said this, I heard her fierce determination slipping away, replaced by despair.

Sheriff Abernathy coughed, breaking the tense silence.

"Let's try to figure out Lani's whereabouts. We must connect the Trophy Killer to her."

My eyes bulged with realization, my mind racing as I connected the dots. The last time I saw Lani was at the diner where Finn first laid eyes on her. There was no way Lani disappeared after an encounter with him, then turned up dead. Another victim of the Trophy Killer. Was Finn the Trophy Killer?

The sheriff's voice jolted me out of my thoughts. "What is it, Everly?"

I struggled to speak, my words tumbling out in a rush. "Lani…her phone. She had plans to meet someone, possibly about a lead on the Trophy Killer."

The sheriff exchanged a glance with Mom for her to elaborate.

Mom sighed and pinched the bridge of her nose. Her face contorted with pain as she spoke. "Lani was studying journalism. She said she was gathering clues to uncover the killer's identity, but I…"

Mocked her, I mentally finished remembering their argument on the night of the party.

"We are working on that cell phone, but it's heavily damaged," the sheriff said. "Did Lani utter any names or locations?" He glanced up at me from his notepad he'd been scribbling in.

My head shook involuntarily as my thoughts continued to churn, consumed by the possibility that Finn could be responsible for Lani's death. I couldn't shake the memory of the humiliation in his eyes when Lani didn't recognize him. The intense anger he must have felt at being deceived. If Finn truly was the Trophy Killer, then my sister died because of me.

ELEVEN

TEARS STREAMED DOWN MY CHEEKS, MY BODY convulsing with sobs. Mom enveloped me in her arms, trying to soothe me and apologize for something she didn't even know I had caused. She would never forgive me if she knew. My entire being shook as I thought about telling her the truth.

"Are we done here?" I heard my mom asking the sheriff, already pulling me up from the chair. My cries drowned out the sheriff's response as Mom guided me out of the station and drove us back home.

———

Strange tapping jolted me awake that night. I blinked rapidly, adjusting to the shadows. The silhouette of a twisted branch was on the window, swaying gently in the breeze—its spindly fingers reaching out and scraping against the glass.

The dark unfamiliar shapes in the room were a blur. But then, like a wave crashing over me, the familiar scent of lavender and chamomile filled my senses. That was Mom's perfume. As I shifted my weight on the soft bed, I felt the warmth emanating from her body next to mine. We lay there together, cocooned in the safety of her bed.

She stirred, her eyes faintly peeking at me. "Are you okay?" Her voice was a croaked whisper.

I forced myself to nod, trying to hide the turmoil inside me. Mom was concerned about my mental state earlier and wanted to take me to the hospital. But I couldn't allow that. The last thing I wanted was for Mom to waste time worrying about me. Lani and all the other victims deserved justice. That's where Graybury's priorities should lie.

She sighed. "Go back to sleep, yeah?" The moonlight cast an eerie glow on her eyes, which seemed to have aged overnight. She brushed a strand of hair from my face, attempting to smile through her pain.

I shut my eyes, allowing myself to relax under her soothing touch. She stroked my hair a few more times before her hand lazily slid down the side of my face and hit the bed. I peeked at her with one eye open. She'd sunk back into the comforting embrace of sleep herself.

She deserved to rest. I, however, had a nagging feeling gnawing in the pit of my stomach—the reminder that there was a wrong I must set right. As much as I wanted to crawl beneath the covers and shield myself from everything, even just for a split second, I knew I couldn't. Sheriff Abernathy took Mom off the Trophy Killer's case. To me, that meant the victims' families had no hope. If my suspicions about Finn were correct, then I needed to steer the authorities in the right direction.

The branch's tapping started up again, almost as if my cue to act. I slipped out of bed quietly, careful not to disturb Mom.

Once in the hall, I crept down the stairs, sticking close to the banister to avoid the spots I knew groaned the loudest. If Mom woke up and found me gone, too... She might assume the worst.

I continued down the stairs, ignoring the picture frames on the wall of Lani and me. The guilt was too much.

The reminder of hiding from Lani the last time I saw her scratched at my heart, threatening to shred it to pieces. I didn't get to say goodbye to her or tell her how much I loved her. Instead, I hid in the kitchen watching the chaotic scene unfold that *I* caused.

I paused on the last stair and dabbed my welling eyes. Creating that profile on MatchBox seemed so harmless in the beginning. I never could have imagined this would be the result. No matter how much I wished for it, there was absolutely nothing I could do to change the past. But I was determined to help catch the person responsible.

Steeling myself for what I was about to do, I took a deep breath and headed out the back door for my bike. Leaves and twigs littered the ground from the thunderstorm. The night air was damp and warm, clinging to me like a shroud as I unlocked the bike and pedaled away from the safety of my home.

Finn did it.

That's all my mind could think. I felt it in my bones. His pain and anger that moment Lani told him off… He probably followed her. Stalked her.

I blinked, forcing my mind not to go to what happened next. I just couldn't…

The looming darkness swallowed me whole as I pedaled faster into the night, to Finn's lake house. Nothing could change my mind, either. With adrenaline pumping through my veins, I was determined to prove Finn's guilt. I wanted solid proof before I uttered his name to the authorities.

A sense of foreboding crept over me as I passed the

woods where they found Lani. Goosebumps prickled my skin. I gripped the handlebars tighter, pedaling fiercely down the slick winding street of Willshire Road.

The lake house stood tall at the end of a long driveway. A blend of wood and stone boasting massive windows that mirrored the glistening lake in the distance. The scenery might've emanated a sense of peace and relaxation, but I couldn't help seeing the ideal place for a house of horrors with its isolation and seclusion.

I propped my bike against a gnarled oak tree. My lungs burned from the exertion as I hurried toward the house, my breaths coming in short, shallow gasps. The sound of my pounding heart filled my ears and my body felt electrified, like I was more animal than human. Every rustle in the nearby bushes made me jump, my senses on high alert, ready to react to any potential danger.

Just stay calm, Everly. You got this.

But the more I thought about it, the more unsure I became. Was my plan really that simple? Just find evidence and take it to the police? What if there was danger waiting for me inside? I didn't have a weapon or anyone who knew where I was. I could end up like the other victims of the Trophy Killer, like... Lani.

The thought made me want to break down into tears once again, but I couldn't let my emotions control me.

Lani had died trying to unmask this murderer and bring justice to the other victims. As much as it scared me, I had to try, too. If there was even a chance of finding clues or evidence in this house, then I had to go inside.

I rounded to the back, searching for a way in. There was an open window on the second floor. Only how would I get up there?

I took a step back, eying the nearby tree, offering a precarious path upwards. Its branches swayed gently in the post-storm breeze. It would have to do.

Beneath the towering tree, I stood trembling with fear and determination. The wind seemed to mock me as I climbed onto the first branch. Ignoring the stinging pain in my hands from the gnarled bark digging into my skin, the slickness of my sneakers on the damp wood, and the burning ache in my muscles, I pushed myself onward. Each step up felt like a fierce battle against Mother Nature herself.

Gasping for air, I finally reached the branch next to the window. My knuckles turned to stone as I grasped onto it with all my might, feeling its rough surface denting into my flesh.

Don't snap, don't snap, I chanted silently, reaching a shaking hand toward the window.

With one last burst of courage, I hauled myself through

the window and into the privacy of Finn's home.

As soon as I plummeted to the floor, the branch I'd been clinging to snapped with a thunderous crack. Immediately, I lay still, listening for any signs of alarm.

Nothing.

I breathed a quiet sigh of relief. That was ridiculously close.

With each passing second, I knew I was crossing a point of no return. Breaking and entering was a crime, for goodness' sake. But desperation had a way with people. And I refused to sit and wait. Abernathy had no clue Finn existed.

I pushed myself up from the floor, taking in my surroundings with wide eyes. There were so many mirrors—full length, like for a dressing room, perhaps. Their gazes were on me accusingly as I stood frozen, wondering what to do next.

A floorboard creaked behind me, and my body went rigid. I whipped around, expecting to find someone there. But I was alone—just my ghostly reflection in the dusty floor mirror. My sunken racoon-like eyes and hollow cheeks were unrecognizable to me. Strands of my short hair stuck out in all directions, some matted with sweat. A lone leaf clung to the corner of my glasses.

With a deep inhale, I shook away my thoughts. None

of that mattered. The task at hand was to prove Finn's guilt. I needed to stay focused and keep a clear head.

I cautiously made my way through the unfamiliar surroundings, inching closer to the exit. The moment I turned the doorknob, the sound of blaring opera music engulfed the air, confirming my theory. The house stood completely isolated. You could scream your lungs out and no one would hear you for miles. A surge of anger soared through me at the possibility Lani might've died within these very walls.

I clenched a fist and continued to the landing where the powerful crescendos carried from below. Who listened to opera that loudly? A serial killer, of course.

There was another odd, rhythmic sound, too. Something akin to aggressive chopping.

I slinked down the carpeted stairs, ducking as low as possible. While the deafening opera obscured any sound I might make, my shadow was still visible.

Then, for some strange reason, a sickening odor filled my nostrils the further I descended the stairs, growing stronger with each step I took. An awful metallic stench, like blood. It was so overpowering I had to cover my nose and mouth with a hand to keep from retching.

What was happening down there?

The chopping sounds continued along with the opera. I

kept against the wall, finally reaching the bottom, too afraid, yet eager to know what was going on. The acrid smell of blood intensified, threatening to make me gag again. I took a slow, steady breath and cautiously peered around the banister.

My insides twisted in disgust as a wave of putrid bile threatened to escape my throat. The stench of death and violence hung heavy in the air, assaulting my senses. I looked on in terror at the bloody drag marks leading to a large pool of congealed blood at a nearby door.

The chopping sounds rang in my ears like a macabre symphony, and a sickening realization dawned on me—Finn must be dismembering another victim. My legs turned to jelly, and I desperately clutched onto the banister for support, trying to hold myself together.

A voice in my head screamed at me to snap out of it, for Lani's sake. I couldn't afford to lose focus now, not when I was this close to catching him in the act.

Catching him in the act…

Quickly, but quietly, I reached into my pocket for my cellphone. Someone needed to see this. Being sure to turn off the light setting, I snapped a few pictures of the crimson trail and texted them to Chance, along with Finn's address.

Gulping, I peered around the corner to the kitchen door which stood slightly ajar. I made out movement inside, someone shuffling around, even humming to the opera. A flash of white stained with blood. That rhythmic chopping. The opera stopped. Silence.

I held my breath, carefully backing out of sight. Somewhere the seconds of a clock ticked noisily.

Then—

My phone pinged.

TWELVE

MY EYES BULGED AS I HURRIED TO MUTE IT. BUT it'd already pinged a couple times more, most likely Chance replying to my text. I heard Finn gasp in the kitchen, aware that he wasn't alone. The door flew open.

"Who's there?" he demanded.

I hurriedly dialed Chance, who answered on the first ring. "Chance, please hurry… *he's going to kill me*." My words hurried out at the sound of Finn's rushing footsteps. Panic clawed its way up my throat as I realized I didn't have Lani's self-defense ring.

I screamed when Finn stopped in front of me.

"What the…?" He blinked confusedly, his white tee shirt stained with blood.

I screamed again, hands outstretched. "The cops are on their way. They know who you are."

Finn's mouth dropped, those gray-blue eyes a mixture of surprise and rage. "How did you get in here?"

A tiny yelp escaped my throat when he grabbed my arm and snatched me up. The phone clattered to the floor.

"Wait a second. Don't I know you?" He squinted at me, his vice-like grip still on my wrist. "The girl from the diner…"

"Please let me go," I whispered.

"What are you doing here? How—?"

"You killed my sister!"

His eyes narrowed as he tugged me closer. "Who are you?"

"I'm—I'm Lani2.0."

Finn let go of me, staggering back as if I'd stabbed him. "You're…" His words choked in his throat. "You catfished me? How did you…? *Why?*" He took a threatening step forward.

I backed against the wall, eyes darting around for an escape route. "Stay back. The sheriff is on his way. They know what you've done."

A sinister smirk crossed his face. "Do you seriously think you can get away with breaking into my house and accusing me of murder?" He hovered over me, glowering.

Suppressing my fear, I stood my ground. My mission was clear—to expose Finn and end his reign of terror.

"I know you're the Trophy Killer, Finn. Your killing spree ends now," I declared.

In the distance, the wailing sirens grew closer, causing a flicker of doubt to cross Finn's face. A rush of relief surged through me, but I remained steadfast in my resolve, refusing to show any signs of weakness.

The police cars pulled into the driveway, their lights cutting through the darkness like a beacon of hope. "It's over, Finn," I said, slowly taking a step toward the door. Finn didn't budge, though his gaze never left me. Picking up my pace, I unlocked the door and barged out into the night, sucking in mouthfuls of the warm air. Sheriff Abernathy and Chance emerged from the vehicles, their expressions confused and concerned.

"Sheriff, you need to arrest him," I said, pointing back at the house. "He killed Lani, and I know there's another victim in there. There's blood *everywhere*."

"Slow down, Everly," the sheriff instructed, his hand resting on his holster. "Tell us what happened."

"Look at him!" I gestured wildly toward Finn, who stood on the porch, his face and clothes smeared with red. "He's covered in blood. And there are bloody drag marks leading into the kitchen. I heard these—these chopping sounds like he was dismembering a body. You have to do something."

The sheriff glared at Finn, at the evidence all over him. "Sir, we're gonna have a look around. Is that all right?"

Finn stood there, stone-faced and emotionless, as he silently nodded his agreement.

Trembling with fear and disgust, I wrapped my arms tightly around myself, unable to even stand the sight of Finn. How had he ever been attractive to me?

The sheriff's voice broke through my thoughts, snapping me back to reality. "Deputy Fuller will stay with you while I go inside and check things out." His gaze then turned to Chance, who met my eyes for the first time since he arrived. I couldn't help but move closer to him as the sheriff and Finn disappeared into the house.

"Everly," Chance hissed at me, his voice laced with anger and worry. "What are you doing here?"

I sighed, knowing I had to tell him the truth eventually. "I broke in."

"You *what?*" Chance's eyes grew wide behind his glasses. "Why?"

"I had a hunch," I said defensively, wrapping my arms tighter around myself.

His eyebrow quirked up in disbelief, clearly wanting more of an explanation. And he was right to expect one—if it weren't for their timely arrival, I might have been in serious trouble.

"He's guilty, okay?" I snapped, upset at both Finn's actions and Chance's interrogations. Annoyed, Chance pressed his lips together in a tight line and shook his head, keeping quiet.

Several minutes later, the sheriff emerged from the house, followed closely by Finn. The expression on the sheriff's face was stern, but not as grave as I'd expected.

"Everly…" He began, pausing in front of me. "I searched that house—top and bottom—there's no one in there."

My jaw dropped as I took a step forward. "But the blood—" I pointed at the house.

"Is from a deer carcass," Sheriff Abernathy interjected, giving me a hard look.

"What?" My eyes flicked between the sheriff and Finn as my world came crashing down. How could that be?

"Roadkill," Sheriff Abernathy said.

"Okay, but was there any evidence inside about those girls' murders?"

Sheriff Abernathy raised his hands in a placating gesture. "Look, there was nothing inside this house that suggests the Trophy Killer lives here." He glared at me, his facial expression more disappointed than accusatory as he handed me back my cell phone. "Everly, I know how you got into Mr. Dunlap's house."

My mouth went dry as we stared at each other in silence for a beat. I still couldn't get over how Finn had fooled him. It was impossible there wasn't a shred of evidence. I just wasn't buying that.

I glared at Finn over the sheriff's shoulder. "And I know *you're* the Trophy Killer," I uttered through clenched teeth.

"All right…" Sheriff Abernathy began, tugging on his belt. "How about we all go down to the station and get this mess sorted out? We must inform your mother, Everly," he added, pointing at me. "She needs to know what happened here. Let's go."

As I lagged Chance to his patrol car, the smell of blood still lingered in my nostrils. The image of those bloody drag marks would haunt my dreams. No way, that was only roadkill.

Chance and I sat in a tense silence, my nerves getting the better of me as we waited for Mom to arrive at the police station. This was uncharted territory for me; my behavior had never warranted a call to my mom before. To make matters worse, it was three o'clock in the morning, adding more pressure to the already stressful situation.

But I wasn't mistaken about Finn. He may have acted

surprised when he found out I created the fake profile, but that didn't mean he was innocent.

Heck no. Not when I recalled all his actions. Ice seemed to flow through his veins as I boldly accused him of taking Lani's life. Not a flicker of emotion crossed his face, and not once did he deny the accusation. He was guilty.

When Mom finally stormed into the interrogation room thirty minutes later, her face was red with fury. "Everly, what the hell?" she demanded, her voice trembling with frustration.

Chance rose from his seat to explain, but before either of us could speak, Sheriff Abernathy entered the room with Finn right behind him.

"I'm sorry I had to call you down here, Sloane," Sheriff Abernathy said sympathetically. "I'm sure you're aware your daughter broke into this gentleman's house tonight…"

Gentleman? Anger welled up inside me because he viewed Finn as innocent, while I was being treated like a criminal for breaking into his house. I glared at him, standing there calmly in a fresh shirt. I wanted to scream at them and demand they test the blood on his old shirt for any evidence tying him to Lani's murder.

But I sat there, seething, while Finn was distant and so

unscathed by all of this. They so should've done more to investigate him.

"Everly, why on earth would you do something like that?" Mom asked. Her tired eyes bored into me.

The truth burned on the tip of my tongue—because he killed Lani. But I held back, unsure of where to begin.

Mom shot a piercing glare at Finn. "Who the hell are you?"

Both he and Sheriff Abernathy looked to me for an answer.

With a heavy sigh, I finally confessed. "Finn is a regular customer at the diner. I—I made a fake dating profile using Lani's identity and chatted with him on MatchBox…"

Mom's eyes bulged with disbelief and horror as she processed my words. The shame washed over me like a tidal wave because what I had to say next would destroy her.

"Mom…" I paused, lip quivering as I gasped for air. "I only broke into his house because I believe he murdered Lani."

"Everly—stop—"

"No, Mom. You didn't see him when—"

"I said stop talking," she warned me sternly. "You manipulated this man and then broke into his house under false pretenses? You're lucky Abernathy hasn't arrested you yet."

"But he *is* the Trophy Killer, Mom," I shot back, my voice rising in desperation. My heart told me Finn was dangerous and if they let him go tonight, another girl would die. I had to make them understand that. I spun to Sheriff Abernathy. "Please, you have to go back to that house. Do not just let him go. Get a cadaver dog or something."

"On what grounds?" Sheriff Abernathy asked. "A fake profile and your gut feeling? That doesn't give you the right to break into someone's house and invade their privacy."

"Everly didn't just go snooping around for no reason," Mom interjected, her tone firm but measured. "She had cause for concern, sheriff. And while her methods were unorthodox, they weren't entirely without merit."

My eyes widened at her. I might've disappointed her, but she knew when to prioritize her job. Did this mean she believed me?

"Unorthodox?" The sheriff snorted. "That's one way to put it. Everly clearly overstepped her boundaries, Sloane. You can't deny that."

"Of course not," Mom conceded, her jaw tight. "I don't condone Everly's actions whatsoever. But let's not forget the larger issue at hand—there's a killer on the loose who targeted us. If you were actually doing your job, my daughter wouldn't have to take matters into her own hands to solve her sister's murder."

Sheriff Abernathy nodded, his face flustered. "We are doing all we can, Sloane, exploring every lead," he assured.

"Good. Then I believe we've wasted enough time already on an overzealous teenager's mistake," Mom said, her eyes landing on me icily.

The silence that followed was thick with tension. As much as I wanted to defend myself, I knew Mom was doing everything in her power to keep me out of trouble.

"Correct," Sheriff Abernathy said. "Mr. Dunlap doesn't wish to press charges. But I'm going to be very clear with you, Everly. You are not to bother him ever again. There is nothing connecting him to any criminal activity, and your actions have only complicated matters. Do you understand?"

I felt like a scolded kindergartener. Why couldn't anybody see through Finn's façade?

"*Everly?*" Mom clipped.

"Yes, sir," I grumbled, catching the pleased expression passing on Finn's face. As badly as I wanted to leap from my seat and hurt him for what he did to Lani, I held my composure.

"Thank you, Abernathy," Mom said, masking her relief with professionalism. "I'll ensure it doesn't happen again."

A short while later, Mom's eyes were two smoldering embers, threatening to ignite into full-blown fury as she stormed around the living room. "Do you have any idea how reckless and dangerous your actions were? Breaking into someone's home? Pretending to be someone else online?" She glared at me accusingly. "Did Lani put you up to that MatchBox nonsense?"

I shook my head and opened my mouth to deny it, but the words died on my lips. I couldn't bring myself to tell her the truth. That I just wanted to get back at Kyle for breaking up with me. How lonely I was without him in this house all by myself. She wouldn't get it. She wouldn't…care.

Yet I needed her to understand the seriousness of the situation with Finn. Another girl would die if we didn't stop him.

"Mom, I know it sounds crazy, but Finn is—"

"Everly—enough!" Her sharp tone sliced the air. "I deal with facts, evidence, and the law. Not your Nancy Drew shenanigans. Your recklessness could tarnish my reputation as county attorney. You are jeopardizing everything I stand for."

I bit my lip, wanting to argue, but knew it was pointless.

"Sheriff Abernathy gave you a warning. You are not to interfere with Finn's life ever again. Now, do I make myself clear?"

"Yes," I nodded, pushing my glasses off my nose. But I was already strategizing my next move.

THIRTEEN

THAT AFTERNOON, I RANSACKED LANI'S messenger bag, my fingers frantically clawing at the worn leather until they finally grasped the manilla folder. My heart leaped with anticipation as I yanked it out and flipped it open. A flurry of crinkled newspaper articles and tattered flyers spilled onto my desk in disarray. Their headlines screaming out a stark reminder of the evil lurking in our small town. Minority girls found savagely murdered.

With quickened breaths, I scanned through the articles frantically, my hands trembling with fear and anger. I was searching for something, any sign of a clue. Then I spotted it amidst the articles—a pattern emerging that pointed to a twenty-mile radius.

I grabbed a notepad and pen and hastily jotted down the victims' families' addresses within biking distance.

Illiana Herrera's mother was on the list. A familiar surge of determination rippled through me as I rushed downstairs where a note from Mom awaited me on the fridge.

Don't forget your dad is picking you up at 3

Good. That left me just enough time to hunt for evidence that pointed to Finn. I knew what Mom and the sheriff had ordered. I was to never bother Finn again. But I couldn't let it go. There was a nagging feeling inside me that said Finn was somehow connected. So, I hatched a plan—a way to prove Finn's guilt without putting Mom's job on the line.

Finn was always at the diner reading those personal ads. Lani's profile couldn't have been the only one he contacted. What if he was using MatchBox as his twisted hunting ground? I needed to talk to the victims' family members. Maybe someone else had a MatchBox profile that connected to Finn. It seemed farfetched, but it was worth pursuing.

I pedaled my way through town excitedly, yet dreading what I might learn. When I used to crave a good mystery, this was not what I had in mind. This wasn't just a game or a puzzle to solve. We were real grieving families, desperate for answers and justice.

Since Lani's death, I kept thrusting myself into the center of it all, the weight of responsibility heavy on my shoulders. My determination to catch this deranged psychopath burned like a fire in my core, fueling my every move.

The Herreras were my first stop. I'd been longing to see Illiana's mother again ever since she barged into Lou's, distraught and afraid.

When I finally rounded the corner and spotted Mrs. Herrera seated in a creaky wooden rocking chair on her porch, my stomach twisted into a knot. My bike slowed to a crawl as I studied her from a distance—her frail figure hunched over in the rocker with a worn cardigan draped over her shoulders. Her eyes fixed on some unseen point, locked in a vacant stare. It was as though she had melded into the porch, a permanent fixture in that one spot for all eternity.

I hopped off my bike and approached her cautiously. "Mrs. Herrera?"

No response. The woman didn't even blink.

"Do you remember me from the diner?" My voice faltered to a desperate whisper. Mrs. Herrera sat there like a living ghost. Her unresponsive gaze seemed to bore holes into my soul.

A flicker of movement caught my eye—a girl standing in the doorway. She emerged from the house quickly, the screen door slamming behind her.

"Get away from my mother… We don't want anything you're selling," she snapped, wiping her hands on a dishcloth. She was identical to Illiana, only around my age. Her dark hair was up in a messy bun.

"I'm so sorry to bother you. I'm here about Illiana," I explained.

"Why?" she demanded, placing a protective hand on her mother's stiff shoulder. Mrs. Herrera continued to stare into the distance, oblivious to the surrounding conversation.

I nervously licked my dry lips, at a loss for words to explain myself. It didn't feel right to barge in and start asking random questions, given the gravity of the situation.

Mrs. Herrera's continuous creaking in her chair filled the awkward silence.

"I'd like to…pay my respects…" I said.

The suspicion faded from the girl's face. "You knew her?" Without thinking, I nodded, though I kept my mouth shut—tasting the bitterness of a lie about to slip off my tongue. The girl's gaze flickered to her unresponsive mother's figure. "You have to excuse her. She's convinced that Illiana will return someday. And she sits here day and night—waiting for her…" Her voice wavered.

"I'm so sorry, really," I said.

She nodded. "We appreciate that. It's been hard since…" She took Mrs. Herrera's limp hand. "We don't know what else to do, where to turn…"

"What is the sheriff saying?" I asked. "Are there any leads?"

She scoffed and rolled her eyes. "He thinks my sister was just another party girl who got mixed up with the wrong crowd."

I uttered a sharp gasp at this revelation, thinking back to the sheriff's promise to me and my mom. What exactly was he doing to solve these murders? Heat flared within me, but I kept my composure for the sake of the Herreras. "That's a shame," I muttered through gritted teeth. "Did Illiana ever use a dating site—like MatchBox?"

Her sister's expression turned sour. "No. Illiana wasn't like that at all. Her focus was on nursing school, not dating. Sure, she had many friends, but…" Her brow creased in skepticism once more. "Where did you say you met my sister?"

"Uh…" My pulse quickened, grasping for an explanation. "Honestly…my older sister knew her. But someone murdered her, too. And I—"

"Well, I'm sure the sheriff is doing everything in his power to find *her* killer," she snapped, crossing her arms defensively.

My hands shook as I pushed up my glasses, a tense silence falling between us. My stomach churned with discomfort and guilt at what she insinuated. She assumed Lani was a white girl. The uncomfortable truth hung in the air, adding to the already heavy knot in my stomach. Because Lani wasn't white. Would that hinder the investigation into her murder?

My heart pounded faster with fear and anger at the terrible realization that my sister's murder may not have the attention it deserved because of the systemic injustices faced by people of color every day. And to make matters worse, Lani was passionate about fighting against this injustice. The irony was suffocating.

"I am truly sorry for your loss," I told them, feeling a lump form in my throat. I turned to leave but paused. "Did your sister know a guy named Finn?"

She furrowed her brow in thought. "Nope. Doesn't ring a bell. Why?"

"Nothing—just wondering." I took one last heart-shattering look at Mrs. Herrera, a hollow shell rocking endlessly in her seat. It was a sobering reminder of the devastating impact the Trophy Killer had on the family members left behind.

Coming here had been a mistake. These people were suffering enough without my intrusive questions and false claims of friendship. All I did was rip open wounds that were trying to heal. Who was I to dredge up such painful memories?

I was just a nosy teenager playing at being a detective, as Mom had said. These were real lives torn apart by loss. I turned away, blinking back tears. Hopping on my bike, I pedaled off.

This killer ripped apart my life, too, though. And unlike everyone else, I was willing to go out and hunt him and see him pay for what he's done.

Next on my list was Travis Carter, the boyfriend of Lichelle Thomas. Lichelle was a stunning twenty-year-old with a rich umber complexion. They found her corpse with the eyeballs gouged from her sockets. The missing body parts, just another cruel and gruesome trophy for the Trophy Killer.

I rode across the cracked pavement, venturing into the grittier part of town. Graffiti-covered walls and boarded-up windows lined the narrow streets, while the scent of car exhaust mingled with that of stale beer from a nearby dive bar. The atmosphere was tense, and more than once, I felt wary eyes on me as I rode past clusters of loitering men who looked like they wouldn't hesitate to cause trouble.

When I neared the rundown house, the roar of motorcycle engines grew louder. A group of bikers gathered around a garage, their laughter echoing through the neighborhood. I parked my bike at a safe distance and marched ahead, trying to mask my apprehension with feigned confidence.

"Excuse me!" I called out over the loud rock music blaring from a radio. "I'm looking for Travis—Travis Carter?"

A tall, leather-clad man with a scruffy beard and sunglasses raised an eyebrow, sizing me up. "Who wants to know?" he asked, his voice deep and gravelly.

I forced myself not to flinch under his menacing presence. "I have some questions about his girlfriend, Lichelle, if he has a moment."

"His dead girlfriend," another biker contorted, climbing onto his bike with a heavy plop. He revved his engine. "And what business is it of yours?"

"It's…very important, actually. Is Travis around?"

The guy on the bike jerked his thumb toward a group of fellows in the garage. "Good luck getting him to talk," he grumbled, his bike roaring ferociously as he sped out of the lot.

I spun and faced the men in the dilapidated garage, all sharing the same rough appearance, their conversation punctuated by guttural laughter. Here it goes, I told myself, marching over.

"Travis?"

The group fell silent, their expressions guarded. The one with the cigarette flicked it to the ground and snuffed it out with his boot. "How do you know me?"

"I don't—I just wanted to speak to you about your girlfriend, Lichelle," I said in a rush. My chest was tight, almost suffocating, as I attempted to appear braver than I felt. I swallowed hard and took the leap. "Did Lichelle ever use MatchBox—the dating site?"

Travis' eyes narrowed as he clenched his fists, the tattoos on his beefy ivory arms seeming to come alive. "What's MatchBox got to do with anything?"

"Well—I believe Lichelle's killer may have connected with her on that site. Did she ever mention a guy named Finn?" I pressed, trying to keep my voice steady despite the intimidating aura radiating from Travis.

"Now wait just a goddamn minute. Are you trying to tell me Lichelle was cheating on me? Is that why she's dead?" His words were like daggers, piercing through my already trembling body.

My mouth hung open in surprise, words failing me.

That was not at all what I meant.

"Who the hell is Finn?" Travis spat, grabbing my arm with a grip so tight I was sure it'd leave a mark.

The answer caught in my throat because Mom would slaughter me. There was no concrete evidence linking Finn to anything, only speculation and desperate attempts to find answers. And twice now, I'd recklessly thrown his name to enraged family members. Stupid, stupid, stupid.

Travis pulled me closer until I smelled the booze on his breath. "Did Lichelle cheat on me with this dude?"

"Please, I'm so sorry," I pleaded, trying to break free. "I wasn't implying an affair—I—"

He released me and left deep imprints of his fingers on my skin. "Get your ass out of here, little girl, before you get hurt."

Without hesitation, I sprinted away until I found my bike, shaking as I hopped on and pedaled furiously. It wasn't until I was several blocks away from the bikers that I finally allowed myself to break down in tears. Fear, anger, and heartache all collided in my mind, making it impossible to think straight. Today had been a complete failure—another dead end in the hunt to prove Finn's guilt. As time ticked by, it seemed less and less probable that he would ever face justice.

FOURTEEN

MY HEART ACHED LIKE A HOLLOW DRUM AS I pedaled through the streets of Graybury, moving on autopilot. Sweat dripped from my body, the sun beating mercilessly on my back. Tears of devastation left salty trails on my face. I focused on the rhythmic beat of my feet against the pedals, pushing myself harder, going nowhere fast. It felt as if I were trying to outrun the pain and the fear that overwhelmed me.

My mind was reeling from the harsh words of Illiana's sister, and a fiery rage simmered inside me. Sheriff Abernathy lied to our faces when he promised to solve this case. His indifference toward the victims and their families showed he didn't care. I felt dumb for being so blind to the injustice that existed in Graybury. Lani tried to warn me, and now she was a victim of this broken system, too.

And I had only the slightest clue what action to take

next, how to set things right. I felt useless.

"Hey, Everly!" someone shouted, jolting me from my turbulent thoughts. It was Benjamin in his truck at the stoplight. I just shook my head, unable to respond. I wasn't ready to be pulled back into reality just yet. The mindless pedaling was enough for now. I picked up speed, the familiar buildings blurring together like watercolors bleeding into one another.

As I rounded a corner, the tires skidded on the gravel. I gaped at the imposing brick building, panting for breath. The sheriff's station. Of course, I'd end up here. With every fiber of my being, I longed for answers—for closure. This place was supposed to provide me with that.

I dismounted my bike with a ball of madness exploding inside me. It was hard enough to cope with my sister's murder, but knowing that her killer was still out there, unpunished, made the pain unbearable. I refused to sit by and become another Mrs. Hererra—an empty vessel, rocking for all eternity.

Bursting through the doors of the station, I hardly registered the startled expressions of the officers and staff as I stormed inside.

"Hey! Tell me what you're all doing to catch the Trophy Killer," I snapped, voice echoing through the room. The words hung in the air like an accusation, drawing the attention of everyone present. The tense silence that followed felt like a noose tightening around my neck, yet I couldn't back down.

"*Answer me.*"

"Everly," a familiar voice called out from behind.

I turned to see Chance approaching, dressed in his police uniform, looking every bit the rookie cop he was. With an eye roll, I pushed up my glasses. "I don't want to speak to you. Where's Sheriff Abernathy, huh?"

"Everly, you don't look so well," Chance said, peering at me closely, at my sweat-soaked sundress and matted hair. He heaved an overwhelming sigh while walking over to the water machine to fill a paper cup. "Here," he held it out to me.

Without a word, I took the cup and guzzled the lukewarm liquid in a few large gulps. "Where is the sheriff?" I repeated, drying my mouth with the back of my hand.

"Let's talk outside," Chance urged quietly, placing a hand on my arm to escort me out, but I squirmed away.

"No. I want some answers, Deputy Fuller. What's the latest development?"

"Everly, please. Storming into the station like this only complicates things for you. I understand you're upset...but this won't change anything." He stared at me, his eyes holding a genuine spark of empathy.

But I didn't care. I was sick of feeling this helplessness. "Then what will, Chance? Because no one here seems to be helping," I yelled over his shoulder at the other deputies.

"Come on." He gave me the gentlest nudge forward.

Outside, the sunlight seemed harsher than before, smoldering even. Chance released my arm and leaned against the station wall, eyeing my bike wearily. "Have you been riding around all day?"

I folded my arms. "I went to see the Herrera family, and they're not happy with the way Illiana's case is being handled, either."

"Everly—?"

"How can you live with yourself knowing you're a part of this corrupt system?"

Chance flinched. He shifted his weight uncomfortably, his gaze flickering to my bike again. "Let me drive you home," he offered, a hint of pleading in his voice.

My legs quivered beneath me as I hesitated, feeling the weight of exhaustion and fatigue overwhelm my body. There was no way I could summon the energy to get back on that bike today. The thought of climbing back onto the seat, pedaling, and enduring more physical strain made me shudder with dread.

I glanced up to protest, but Chance was already picking

up my bike and heading to his truck.

"Twelfth and Oak, right?" he called over his shoulder.

"Yes," I answered softly, following behind him, legs wobbling like Jello. I couldn't deny that I appreciated his offer.

Chance hiked my bicycle in the back and opened the passenger door for me. I collapsed onto the seat with a heavy sigh.

The truck hummed with a low, steady vibration as it navigated the uneven streets of Graybury. My fingers absentmindedly traced the frayed seam on the edge of the seat, grateful the A/C was on full blast. I cut my eye at Chance, at the way he gripped the wheel with an intensity that matched my own feelings.

"You asked me before why I stayed with the department," he blurted.

I turned my gaze to him fully, curious, yet also taken aback he brought that up so candidly.

"Graybury..." he sighed, his grip on the steering wheel relaxing slightly. "This town is broken in so many ways, and the police department is no exception. But if there's one thing I've learned from my time here, it's that change can only come from within." He glanced at me briefly before returning his attention to the road. "I stay because I believe change is possible. It won't happen unless there are people on the inside who genuinely care about making it happen. And…" he hesitated, body tensing all over again. "I must be careful, play by their rules for now. If I want to make a difference, I can't afford to lose my job."

My gaze lingered on his face, scanning for any hint he was just feeding me BS. But all I found was raw honesty and a strong sense of conviction. Despite my urge to challenge his belief that he had to play by the system's rules, I couldn't deny the hard truth—Chance would be powerless if they were to fire him.

He straightened in his seat, squaring his shoulders. "I know I'm just an eighteen-year-old kid," he said modestly, his attention focused on the road ahead. "But I do hope to climb the ranks someday. Not for power or recognition, but because I believe that I can make a difference—that I can help set things right in this twisted town."

A strange sensation came over me as the truck rumbled over the bumpy road. I turned my head back to my window to shield my emotions. All my pent-up anger had melted away, replaced by a newfound respect for Chance. For the first time since this all started, a sense of calmness washed over me. I shut my eyes to revel in the moment, savoring every peaceful second.

Finally, I found the words to speak. "I—I'm sorry for what I said earlier."

The truck slowed to a stop in front of my house, the engine humming softly as Chance glanced over. The weight of everything that had transpired hung heavily between us.

He offered me a small, rueful smile. "I understand you, Everly. But please know that we're on the same side." He placed his warm hand on top of mine, a comforting weight that reminded me I was not alone at this moment. His touch was tender and understanding, offering silent support and reassurance. But he pulled away after a beat.

I nodded, swallowing hard against the lump in my throat, before blurting out my request. "Can you check out Finn Dunlap again—just to make sure he's not involved in anything shady," I added quickly.

Chance's expression shifted, a flicker of concern knitting across his brow. He let out a slow sigh, weighing his options. "Abernathy already looked into Finn. He warned you not to pursue this further."

"True—but you didn't investigate Finn. And I trust you, Chance, over the sheriff." I shifted, folding my arms across my chest. "If it's up to Abernathy, Lani's murder will go unsolved like the Trophy Killer's other murders have."

"I promise you that won't happen, Everly. But...I'm gonna need you to stop interfering. If Sloane finds out what you did today..."

I spun to him quickly, but he raised his hands in mock defense. "No worries—my lips are sealed." He pretended to zip his mouth shut, making me smile.

Filled with gratitude, I said my thanks as I climbed out of the truck. I retrieved my bike and started up to the house, not before stealing a quick glance at Chance, offering a small wave of appreciation. His warm smile and reassuring presence had made all the difference in my day.

My day...

Dad would be here any minute to pick me up. I rushed up the stairs, purposely ignoring the uneasy feeling in my gut at the thought of him. The last conversation we had was a blur, yet here he was, showing up when my life was in shambles.

"Great timing, Dad," I muttered, entering my bedroom. Immediately, I peeled my sundress away from my clammy skin. Ugh, I was such a dirty mess. And so was my desk. I gaped at the clutter. Lani's messenger bag lay open, its contents strewn about like morbid confetti, remnants of my chaotic search for answers.

I carefully stacked the papers, my heart aching with every sheet I touched. The haunting faces of the victims— so young, their lives cut short in the most brutal way imaginable. I couldn't stand the grainy black-and-white newspaper images hardly sharing any details. These victims deserved so much more than this. I counted six victims. Lani was number seven.

As I stuffed the paper back into the messenger bag, I had to drill it into my head that I wasn't turning my back on these girls. This wasn't over. Today was a bust, but tomorrow was a new day.

I picked up the messenger bag to place the clippings back inside, and my hand brushed against something unexpected—a small, wrapped journal. It was bound in tattered leather and secured with a fragile-looking ribbon.

Curiosity piqued, I began unwrapping the surrounding fabric, and paused, wondering if I should respect Lani's privacy. But with Lani gone and the possibility that this journal could hold vital clues, I couldn't afford to ignore it, right?

I sighed. "Forgive me, sis." Unraveling the ribbon, I opened the journal to a bookmarked page, my eyes widening as they took in the hastily scribbled notes and theories about both the Graybury Slayer and the Trophy Killer.

"Lani…" I whispered, gazing at the list of connections between the victims running down the side of the page. She underlined the words time and patterns multiple times, accompanied by various dates and locations. I turned the page to more cramped handwriting and doodles. It was a bunch of random thoughts and possibilities. I didn't have the time to sort through it all now, but definitely later. The journal flipped back to the bookmarked page. Just as I was about to put the book away, I noticed two names scrawled hastily off the edge of the paper, as if an afterthought or revelation. My trembling fingers traced over the names—Arthur and Jeffrey, my dad's name.

FIFTEEN

I PUSHED MY FORK AIMLESSLY THROUGH THE lettuce and croutons of my once-appetizing Caesar salad, now left uneaten because of mounting unease. The buzz of conversation and clinking silverware filled Lou's Inn, but it all blurred in my peripheral vision as I struggled to focus on the man sitting across from me—my dad. It had been an eternity since I last saw him, and now that he was finally here, all I could see was his name scribbled on a crumpled piece of paper—next to details about a notorious serial killer. I had no time to process any of it in the moment because I had to get ready for this lunch.

"I'm really glad we got the chance to do this today," Dad said. He reached for my hand but stopped short, his fingers hovering over the table. "You haven't taken a bite. Is something the matter with your food?"

"Nope," I answered, unable to keep the hesitation from

seeping into my voice. How could I concentrate on small talk when all I wanted was to confront him about that strange discovery? Demand some answers. But my courage faltered under his steady gaze, my dad, already reaching for another topic, a way to connect with me after so many months apart.

"Sloane tells me you're working here—how do you like it?" he said, attempting to bridge the chasm between us with small talk about my job, of all things. A job I didn't particularly care for, but he wouldn't know that because he isn't a part of my life.

It took all my willpower not to jump up and storm out of that diner. "It's just a first job…" I stabbed a cherry tomato with my fork, sneaking a glance at him adjusting his glasses, nervously. His wide, dark eyes—the same as my own—were sad. But I didn't care. I didn't care that this lunch was important to him. There were plenty of important moments in my life, and he was nowhere to be found. I should've followed his example and bailed on this stupid lunch, just as he'd done all my life.

He ran a hand through his raven hair, desperately trying to break the tension. "Remember that bakery we used to go to? The one with the cinnamon rolls you couldn't resist. Maybe we could pop in there afterwards and grab a roll or two." He jumped his eyebrows in a playful attempt.

But it was not working. Cinnamon rolls could not fix the brokenness in our relationship.

I shook my head.

"Listen, kiddo—I know haven't been around much lately…" he trailed off, his gaze flickering out the window beside us. "But I'm here for you. If there's anything you'd like to talk about…"

He couldn't even look me in the eye when he said this because he knew it was a lie. Insulting even. We both knew the truth—his job would always come first. It was no telling when I'd see him again, so we'd better discuss why his name was inside Lani's journal.

As if he'd read my mind, he said, "Do you want to talk about Lani? I'm really sorry about what happened to her."

I sucked in a sharp breath, struggling not to roll my eyes. How dare he use my dead sister as an excuse for our lack of connection? The nerve of him.

Unable to take it anymore, I dropped my fork with a loud clink against my plate and gripped the corners of the table to stand. But then déjà vu hit as Kyle and his girlfriend walked into the diner, glued to the hip—all smiles and giggles. I sank back into my seat, completely numb, feeling trapped and hopeless in this too small, claustrophobic town.

I could not handle this today. Not now.

I rubbed my temples, attempting to will away the thoughts I didn't want. But it was no use. The memories were like a swarm of bees in my mind, buzzing and stinging relentlessly. Memories of Kyle and I, Dad's sudden reappearance, Lani's unsolved murder, the looming presence of a serial killer…

My insides twisted with anxiety and nausea, threatening to spit up the morsels I'd managed to eat. Maybe I was sick. I could tell Dad that and he could take me home and go back to wherever he came from.

A spark of excitement ignited in Dad's eyes as he spotted Kyle, unaware of the recent breakup between us. "Hey—isn't that your boyfriend?" he asked eagerly. "Want to invite him over?"

"No," I murmured. As badly as Dad longed for someone to come and rescue him from this awkward reunion, Kyle was not the answer.

Dad sat up straighter in his seat as they strolled by, a small smile on his face. I kept my gaze fixed out the window, but I could sense Dad preparing to greet them. Yet Kyle continued walking, ignoring our presence entirely.

While part of me was relieved he didn't force a conversation with my dad, I couldn't help but get mad at his lack of condolences for Lani's death. His actions only added to the growing list of reasons why we were better off apart.

"Are you sure you don't want to invite him over?" Dad asked. "Don't let me scare him away…" he uttered a nervous laugh. But I was sick of it.

"Dad—just stop—"

"Honey, what's wrong? You can tell me."

"You can't possibly expect me to pour my entire life out to you over a stupid fifteen-minute lunch. Everything is falling apart, and you don't even know it." I scoffed. "What does it matter? Once your plate is clean, you're going to disappear again anyway, so just go already."

His entire body sagged as his face twisted into a mask of guilt. "Everly, I never wanted to be the father who constantly disappoints you, always absent because of my job." His voice broke as he struggled to find the right words. "But sometimes life doesn't give us what we want. Being a sheriff means being accountable for an entire town's safety. It's not an excuse, it's the harsh reality." His eyes glistened with unspoken regret as he held back tears.

I gazed at him, truly taking in his appearance—the deep lines of exhaustion etched like scars on his face. The warmth and joviality I had known from my childhood had faded from his eyes, now replaced with a heavy sense of burden and resignation. It couldn't have been easy for him to be sheriff, especially considering my disappointment with Abernathy's actions. My mind flashed to Mrs. Hererra. As much as I resented Dad's absence and abandonment, if it meant keeping his town safe so that no other mother would have to fear for their daughters, then perhaps it was worth the sacrifice. But why couldn't he protect me right here in Graybury?

"I understand that," I said. "But—can't you take over as sheriff here? Abernathy is doing a poor job of investigating these murders. And now Mom is off the case because of a conflict of interest…" I made air quotes on that remark. "I really don't trust Abernathy," I whispered.

Dad sighed heavily. "This town—" he shook his head. "I could never be Graybury's sheriff. But…" He reached across the table and took my hand. "You could come back to Wood River with me," he suggested, his tone hopeful. "I know you would love it there. The schools are great— you could meet new people, make new friends…"

I'd never allowed myself to imagine life outside of Graybury. But now, as I looked around at the same old sights and faces, I felt more stuck than ever. Especially when my gaze landed on Kyle sitting in our old booth with his new girlfriend. Maybe a fresh start was what I needed to move on. The idea tugged at me, but I quickly pushed it away.

Move on? What was I thinking? How could I move on when Lani's killer was still out there? How could I even think about leaving Mom to deal with the aftermath alone?

Without even realizing it, I had pulled my hand from Dad's grasp. "I can't," I said firmly. "I won't just forget about Lani and run away. We need closure before we can go forward." My resolve solidified the more I thought of all the unanswered questions and unfinished business that still loomed over this little town. Leaving was not an option.

Dad nodded understandably, eyes lowering to his plate as he picked around at his food, too.

I fidgeted with the corner of a napkin as I spoke. "You know, Dad, ever since Lani's murder, I am consumed with trying to connect the dots with this copycat killer," I admitted. He raised a brow, waiting for me to explain more, so I continued. "I need to understand why he did it. Who he is. What drives him to collect these gruesome mementos. Why we had to suffer." I pushed aside a leaf of lettuce, hesitating. "I found your name scribbled somewhere, next to another name—Arthur."

Surprise flickered across his face. "Arthur Frye? Now that's a name I haven't heard in years," he said, smiling painfully. "Arthur was my first partner, back when I was an officer. We worked together on some tough cases, including the Graybury Slayer's case..." His words trailed off, his gaze drifting beyond the walls of the small diner as if reliving memories long gone. "That case changed everything for all of us—especially Arthur."

"What happened to him?"

"Arthur was a brilliant criminal profiler. He had an uncanny ability to delve into the mind of a killer and understand their motives and methods. However, it was a treacherous path to tread, one that consumed him as we delved deeper into the Graybury Slayer's case. We'd never dealt with a serial killer before. And the horrors we encountered, the shattered lives of the victims' families, took a toll on us all.

"Arthur ended up finding solace in the bottom of a bottle. Night after night, he drowned himself in whiskey until he was unrecognizable. He was no longer of use to us, so we had to let him go." He said this as if I needed convincing.

"By the time we caught the Graybury Slayer, Arthur was a shadow of the man he once was. He'd lost everything—his career, his family, his... friends..." He swallowed hard, guilt etching deep within his features, probably blaming himself for not being able to save his partner.

"Last I heard about Arthur was he attempted suicide." Dad's voice trembled as he spoke, his eyes glistening.

"I'm sorry, Dad," I whispered, my heart aching for him. I hadn't meant to bring up such painful memories. But now it made sense why Lani had written their names in her journal. She must have planned to question them about the Graybury Slayer, but never got the chance. In that moment, I wished I could ask Dad what she wanted to know.

Dad's expression was regretful as he continued. "Suicide and depression looms over the world of law enforcement—especially when one doesn't seek the proper help. That's why I can't stay here, Ev. This town is a haunting reminder of..." He trailed off, unable to finish his sentence. Then suddenly, his eyes bored into mine, filled with genuine concern. "I know you want closure but trust me—you don't want to open the door to obsessing over a monster. Being inside the mind of a serial killer is a dangerous place."

My body trembled at his words, but it still wasn't enough to prevent me from pursuing this killer.

SIXTEEN

IT WAS BEAUTIFUL—HOW BRIGHTLY THE SUN shone in a clear blue sky, casting its warm, golden rays upon Graybury. It was the kind of summer day that seemed to make everything come alive, from the vibrant green leaves on the trees to the gentle hum of bees collecting nectar from the blossoms. The weather held a bittersweet reminder of Lani's vivacious spirit. She hated the rain—said it only brought gloom and sadness. The irony of it all stung like a fresh wound as I glanced around at Lani's friends—people I didn't know— gathering to enter the church in a sea of peach colored clothing, Lani's favorite color.

It didn't appear to be a funeral at all, as everyone paid honor to Lani's bright and cheery nature. I smoothed my hands down my belted shirt dress, the same shade of pink as everyone else's attire.

The only person who didn't seem to fit in was Gus, with his loud Hawaiian-style shirt that clashed against our pale pinks. He stood casually with his hands in his pockets, trying to charm a trio of attractive girls nearby. I couldn't help rolling my eyes.

Why was he here? Lani didn't even like him.

"Hey, Ev," a voice whispered beside me. I turned to see Benjamin, and my heart broke at the pain on his face. He nibbled on his lip nervously, his eyes glistening.

Without hesitation, I threw my arms around him. He squeezed me tight for a beat, and then immediately let go to compose himself. We shared a nod of understanding.

I took a shaky breath, trying not to work myself up. The night before, I'd lain in bed staring at the ceiling, trying to prepare myself mentally for what was to come. I knew we would have to lay Lani to rest eventually. Honestly, I was glad. I couldn't bear the thought of her lying in that cold morgue all alone.

As we took our respectful places inside the church, I kept my eyes on everything but the casket ahead. There was no way I could sit there calmly, knowing Lani was lying in a wooden box just feet from me, that she was never coming back.

The priest began the eulogy. My eyes darted to my

parents beside me. I was grateful Dad stayed in Graybury for the funeral. His presence was a tiny comfort in the face of overwhelming grief, even though he and Mom hardly acknowledged each other throughout the ceremony. The tension between them was palpable, like an invisible wall that separated them despite their physical proximity. It was clear they were trying to be civil for Lani's sake, but the trauma of their strained relationship seeped like a poisonous gas.

Mom's face was sorrowful, her eyes red-rimmed and glistening with unshed tears. Dad stared straight ahead, jaw clenched, his expression unreadable.

"Lord, we gather here today to celebrate the life of Lani, a cherished daughter, sister, and friend," the priest said, his voice echoing through the hushed church. He continued speaking words of comfort and hope, but I couldn't concentrate. My attention wandered farther around the room, catching Sheriff Abernathy, Chance, and a few other deputies huddled near the back of the church. Anger rose within me at the thought of Abernathy's incompetence in catching Lani's killer. Had he done something about Illiana's murder, we wouldn't be here today. My sister wouldn't be dead.

The priest droned on in the background as I battled with myself to stay put. I really did want to leap from the pew and tell Abernathy to go out and do his job. The Trophy Killer might have another victim at that very moment.

Unable to allow my mind to go there, I shifted my focus back to the priest. Today was about Lani.

But I stared past the priest to the stained-glass window, an image of a saint bathed in colorful light. I struggled to pay attention, my mind consumed by the possibility of Finn's involvement.

Without thinking, I pulled out my phone to text Chance. I kept my phone hidden beneath the folds of my dress as I typed.

Any word on Finn?

The congregation stood to sing a hymn, their voices blending in a haunting melody. I gently swayed along, sneaking glances at my screen. Finally, Chance texted back.

Now is not the time, Everly

Then when was? I snapped my neck around to eye him.

"Everly?" Mom hissed harshly, glaring at my phone.

"Sorry," I mouthed, sticking my phone back into my pocket. The priest was speaking about Lani's bright spirit and unwavering kindness, but it all just felt phony to me. He didn't know Lani. He was only saying nice things because he was supposed to. Even as I watched Mom nodding along, I felt irritated. She didn't exactly appreciate Lani's true nature either.

But that didn't mean she didn't love her daughter, my conscious argued, my shoulders sagging in sorrow. I was just bitter. All of this was so wrong. Lani should not be lying here dead, while her killer still roamed free, breathing the same oxygen as me.

A half hour later, a solemn silence hung in the air as the priest concluded the eulogy. The room seemed to close in when it was time to shuffle to the front of the church. My feet dragged reluctantly across the worn carpet as I followed Mom to the casket.

There Lani lay, looking… different. It didn't seem like my sister at all. The wig perched atop her head was brunette and cropped and a poor substitute for my sister's once-luxurious, long hair. The makeup wasn't Lani's type at all, either. She would've never worn that shade of lipstick.

"Everly, I know it's hard," Mom began, noticing my expression, but I hardly heard her as my gaze was now fixed on Lani's neck.

"Those marks…" I whispered, reaching a trembling

hand out to move away the collar of her dress.

"Everly, stop—" Mom warned, but it was too late. The realization came crashing down on me like a tidal wave, drowning me in a sea of rage and despair. Ligature marks.

"He—he strangled her?" I spun to my mother and screamed. My voice echoed through the hallowed chamber. But I didn't care. The concerned stares, the shame burning in Mom's eyes, the crushing weight of my grief. None of that mattered. All that consumed me was the need for justice. I wanted somebody to pay for this.

"Baby, calm down," Mom pleaded, reaching for me. She glanced at Dad to do something, but I tore away from her grasp. I needed to get away from there. Angry tears blurred my vision as I stomped down the aisle, fingers clenching and unclenching like a caged animal. Stopping in front of Sheriff Abernathy and Chance, my shoulders rose and fell as I struggled to find words. Meeting their intense gazes, I felt a burning rage within me, but said nothing. Instead, I stormed past them, burst out the doors, and sprinted away with no destination in mind—I just needed to escape. My legs kept pumping until giving out at the park a block away. Sinking into the grass, I gulped the sultry summer air in mouthfuls, heaving an ugly, angry sob.

No one deserved that—especially not my sister.

It felt as if my heart had grown sharp nails and was trying to claw its way out of my chest.

I was extremely desperate for any shred of evidence that could get this case moving. And then, as if the universe heard me, Chance texted.

Meet me at Lou's Inn

The bell clanged loudly as I snatched the diner door open a short while later. Aside from a few older gentlemen at the counter, perched on stools sipping coffee, Lou's was empty. I spotted Chance immediately, sitting straight ahead at the booth in the back. His dark eyes locked onto mine.

Huffing exasperatedly, I marched over and slapped my palms on the table, hovering over him. "Tell me you have something."

"Well…" Chance began, rubbing the back of his neck, glancing around for anyone within earshot. "I've been digging into Finn's background, searching for a connection." He leaned closer to me, so close I smelled his woodsy cologne. Voice low and cautious, he said, "I found out his aunt's boyfriend was Matthias Young's cellmate."

My eyes widened, plopping into the seat opposite him.

My mouth hung open, but I didn't know what to say. So many thoughts swam around in my head.

"Wait, I didn't know Finn was from Graybury."

"His family isn't. Just the cellmate. And it's his aunt by marriage so…the connection may be a little tenuous."

I rubbed my temples with both hands, desperately trying to piece this all together. "Do you think the cellmate is like an accomplice or something? Or do you think Finn got his twisted ideas from the Graybury Slayer's cellmate?"

"I—don't know which angle to pursue first," Chance said cautiously. "But I will investigate them all before I present this to Abernathy."

"Wait—"

"Everly. I can't just blurt this idea out to the sheriff without anything concrete to back it up. Give me just a little more time to—"

"Time is not on our side, Chance," I snapped. "What if another girl dies?"

Chance sucked in a sharp breath and clenched his jaw. "Don't you think I'm worried about that, too? But I can't risk being the person responsible for jeopardizing any potential case against this guy."

I stared out the window at nothing, attempting to tamp down my frustration. Chance was right, but that did little to soothe my burning desire for justice. "So, what is the next move?"

"That's classified information. I shouldn't have even shared this, but I want you to know that I'm doing everything in my power. I will not stop pursuing this until we capture him, understand?" He reached across the table and placed his hand on top of mine. "And if you ever need someone to talk to, you have my number."

I glanced down at his hand, his touch warm and comforting as a cozy blanket.

Asha appeared at our table, and Chance pulled away. "Can I… get you two anything?" she asked, sensing our tension.

My body trembled with pent-up frustration as I stood up abruptly, unable to bear the situation any longer. "Actually, I'm just leaving," I snapped. Chance's lips parted in protest, but I ignored him and uttered a cold goodbye before storming out.

The waiting game, the feeling of helplessness, the constant paranoia and fear—it was all too much for me to handle. As Chance had pointed out, he shouldn't be telling me anything about the case. Just that small bit of info about the cellmate was enough to drive me mad. It was our only connection to the serial killer, but stupid protocols and regulations prevented us from acting.

The frustration clawed at my insides, picking away my sanity. I needed to let go of this obsession, to leave it in the hands of the authorities. The more I tried to pursue it on my own, the more it consumed me. And to make matters worse, I couldn't even say a proper goodbye at my sister's funeral. It was time to walk away from it all. Let Abernathy and his team handle it. I was done.

When I got home, I planned to take a hot bath. Just sit there and soak until my fingers turned pruney.

But as I approached my front stoop, my eyes landed on a small brown package sitting on the bottom step. Scrawled in squiggly black writing was my name: **EVERLY**.

There was no return address or any indication of who might have left it.

Maybe it was from Dad. I knew he was going back to Wood River as soon as the funeral was over, and who knew when I'd see him again. Yet he asked me to join him, I reminded myself.

Maybe I should take him up on his offer after all—and get as far away from Graybury as possible.

Once inside the house, I headed straight for the kitchen for a pair of scissors to slit the tape. The package was so light it felt empty in my hands.

As the cardboard fell away, a choked gasp slipped from me, and I dropped the box as if it were on fire. Inside, nestled among a crumpled newspaper, and stained with dried blood, lay a single sawed-off finger.

SEVENTEEN

I held a trembling hand over my mouth while reading the MatchBox text. It came through seconds after discovering the grisly contents inside the package. Fighting against the urge to gag, I turned my attention back to the screen, realizing that this was the Trophy Killer, taunting me because he knew my real identity. But how?

My thumb hovered over the phone's screen, uncertainty and fear gripping my insides. I wanted to text back, to demand his identity, but I couldn't bring myself to respond. It felt as if paralysis had taken over me.

The killer had found me, but how? Was he watching me now?

Adrenaline burst through me as I rushed to the nearest window. I peeked out the drawn shade, my eyes darting back and forth, scanning for any sign of movement or someone lurking. The eerie silence only heightened my senses. The trees cast long shadows across the yard that seemed to morph into a sinister figure waiting to pounce.

Unable to bear it any longer, I stepped away from the window, my legs giving out beneath me. I sank to the floor and wrapped my arms around my knees, trying to steady my breathing. I attempted Chance's breathing technique, but it was no use. The overwhelming fear was suffocating. I squeezed my eyes shut against the throbbing pain in my chest.

Rocking back and forth, I hugged my knees tighter, Mrs. Herrera and her rocking chair flashing in my mind.

But I shook my head against that thought. No. I couldn't become like her. I had to be brave for... I paused; my back straightened.

Oh no. It can't be.

All ten of Illiana Herrera's fingers had been severed.

With a shaky hand, I reached for the package again, sneaking one last peek at the grotesque contents, at the chipped pink polish on the fingernail. And I knew the horrifying truth—that was one of Illiana's fingers.

Clenching my jaw, I fought back the urge to vomit. I

needed to focus and try to piece all of this together.

Finn hadn't known I was Lani2.0 until I confessed at his house. And now, the killer has sent me one of his trophies, dragging me further into his twisted game. This had to be Finn; I just knew it. And if this package wasn't proof, then I didn't know what was.

The sun had set by the time I rolled to a stop at Finn's house. To hell with my orders to leave him alone. I needed this resolved, no matter what the consequences. Handing over this critical evidence to Sheriff Abernathy was a fleeting thought, because I didn't trust him. Even my faith in Chance wavered. But that didn't matter anymore. This killer's twisted game of cat and mouse had pushed me past the point of no return. He wanted me to unmask him, even relishing my inability to do so.

Either way, nothing was going to stop me from confronting Finn about this package.

My heart raced with determination as I tore up the gravel pathway, my bike abandoned behind me. My fists clenched tightly around the gruesome package as I pounded on Finn's door with all my might.

"Open up, Finn!" I yelled, taking a step back to survey the dark house. A shadow flitted across a window on the second floor, confirming that Finn was inside. I waited for him to answer, eager for a confrontation.

A few moments later, heavy footsteps echoed down the stairs and Finn appeared on the other side of the door, his phone pressed to his ear. "Yes, sir, she's here now. Please hurry," he spoke into the phone before hanging up and turning his menacing gaze toward me.

"The sheriff is on his way," he snarled, pointing a finger at me. "If you don't leave right now, they will arrest you."

Knowing I was in the right, I stood my ground. "The only person who needs to be arrested is you, Finn, you disgusting monster. You send me one of your sick trophies and expect me to stay silent? I can't wait for Abernathy to come."

His face paled at my words, and for a moment, I saw a flicker of guilt in his eyes. But then he shook his head, his expression hardening. "You are out of your mind. Now leave!"

"Or what, Finn? You're gonna kill me next?"

The door flew open with a deafening bang, and I stumbled backward in shock, missing the last few stairs. Pain shot through my ankle as it twisted beneath me, but I couldn't tear my eyes away from Finn's stare. He stood there, his body rigid and tense, his piercing eyes locked onto me with an unwavering intensity that sent chills down my spine. His clenched jaw betrayed his inner struggle, making me wonder what he was about to do next. But he remained frozen.

Sheriff Abernathy pulled up shortly thereafter. "Everly, I'll be damned," he huffed, emerging from the patrol car. Chance climbed out of the passenger seat. He gave me a *what's going on* expression.

My hands trembled as I thrust the box into Sheriff Abernathy's hands. "You have to arrest Finn," I cried, my voice raw with fear and anger. "He sent me this."

The air seemed to thicken around us as both Abernathy and Chance peered inside the box. They reacted the same as I did upon the discovery.

"What the hell is this?" Sheriff Abernathy demanded, jerking back. Chance held a fist to his mouth as if he, too, was forcing down his vomit.

I glared at Finn, my arms folded tightly across my chest. "Why don't we ask him?"

Finn's eyes widened in panic, but he didn't speak.

"Is this even real, Everly?" Sheriff Abernathy turned to me, doubt creeping into his tone.

"Of course, it's real," I snapped. "And I'm pretty sure it belongs to Illiana Herrera." I pointed accusingly at Finn. "He sent me one of his trophies."

"Jesus Christ," Finn uttered under his breath, running a

hand through his hair in distress.

I turned back to Sheriff Abernathy. "He is the Trophy Killer, sheriff, and I can prove it. His aunt's boyfriend…" I paused, glancing at the disbelief crossing Chance's face, but I had to bring this to Abernathy's attention. I had to expose Finn once and for all. "He was Matthias Young's cellmate. That's Finn's connection to the serial killer."

Sheriff Abernathy glanced at Chance and took a double look. "Were you aware of this?"

Before Chance could respond, Finn's face contorted with rage. "Get this girl off my property—now!"

"Sir, did you send this package to Everly?" Sheriff Abernathy asked sternly, though we all knew Finn would never admit to anything.

I rolled my eyes in frustration at Abernathy's incompetence. Such a joke.

"I don't know what's in that box or how it got there," Finn growled. "But if she doesn't leave my property right now, I want her arrested for trespassing."

Sheriff Abernathy let out a defeated sigh. "Fine. Everly, get your bike—you're coming with us to the station."

My heart pounded in my chest as I realized this could be my last chance to expose Finn.

Pissed was an understatement to explain how I felt, once again, sitting across from Abernathy, his stony gaze drilling into me as if I were the criminal. And once again, Finn was nowhere to be seen, untouched and unbothered by the ordeal. How much longer would this charade continue, with Abernathy refusing to do his job?

"Are you kidding me, Everly?" Mom demanded when she burst into the interrogation room. The flickering fluorescent light above made the lines on her face seem more prominent, her mouth a tight line of worry and agitation. "You left your sister's funeral to do this?"

Her words slapped me hard in the face. That wasn't my intention at all.

"Sloane, we have another problem," Sheriff Abernathy said, and proceeded to show her a photo. "Everly brought this to us."

Mom's face morphed into utter disgust. "A chopped off finger?"

"The killer left that on our porch, addressed to me," I said.

"But why would the killer suddenly change his MO and send you a trophy? Why you, Everly?" Sheriff Abernathy asked skeptically.

I felt my blood boiling at the insinuation. Did he seriously think that I may have chopped off someone's finger and left it on my doorstep?

Mom glared at him in distaste. "That's for you to get off your ass and figure out, Abernathy. This psycho is targeting my daughters because of Matthias Young. He's already taken Lani from us and now he's tormenting Everly. I want that son of a bitch's head on a platter."

"Mom—it's Finn—" I tried to interject, but her sharp gaze made my words choke in my throat.

Her attention focused back on the sheriff. "I want a unit stationed outside my house."

Sheriff Abernathy nodded. "Of course. And maybe it would be best for someone to keep an eye on you as well," he said pointedly, looking straight at me.

Mom scoffed. "It's easier for you to blame a kid than to do your job properly."

Sheriff Abernathy raised his hands defensively. "Come on, Sloane, you know protocol. I have to explore all possibilities, ask tough questions…"

"Well, you're barking up the wrong tree. There's no way in hell Everly magically obtained a severed finger to parade around. Run the DNA, track where the package came from, do your job, and *find* the sick bastard." She came over and grabbed my arm, pulling me out of my seat. "We're leaving."

But the sheriff's voice stopped us in our tracks. "One

more strike against Finn, and I'll have to arrest you, Everly. You're on thin ice."

Mom's grip tightened around my arm. "Let's go."

Outside, the shadows cast by the streetlights seemed to stretch and contort, looming over us like menacing phantoms as I quickly shoved my bike into the back of Mom's SUV. Her voice trembled with fury as she ordered me to get into her car. I complied, sliding into the passenger's seat as she got behind the wheel.

As soon as the doors slammed shut, she rounded on me. "What the hell is your obsession with this guy?"

"Mom, his aunt's boyfriend was the Graybury Slayer's cellmate," I explained desperately.

"And?"

"It's a connection between Finn and the serial killer, isn't it?"

"Not a connection worthy of an arrest," she cried, her voice rising to a shrill pitch. She took a deep breath while rubbing the bridge of her nose. "Ev, I don't doubt your intelligence or your resourcefulness," she admitted, her voice heavy with concern. "But you're not a detective. You're my daughter, and you're all I have left," she said, placing her hand tenderly on my cheek. "I can't bear the thought of losing you, too." She paused for a moment before continuing in a choked voice.

"This serial killer is targeting me—I won't let you run around town putting yourself at risk. Once we have that officer stationed outside our house, there are going to be some changes. You are to come straight home after work, Everly. No more harassing Finn or poking around for answers. Do you understand how serious I am?" She clamped a hand on my shoulder, forcing me to look her in the eye.

I nodded, refusing to argue. Because no matter who sat outside the house, the killer could still contact me through MatchBox.

EIGHTEEN

SEVEN DAYS. SEVEN DAYS OF SILENCE SINCE I'D heard any new information about the case. Not a peep from Mom. No more trips to the station with Abernathy. Chance was no longer answering my texts. Even the killer himself had gone eerily quiet. But that was likely because of the cop sitting outside the house every evening. Or maybe this was just the calm before another storm.

I couldn't afford to let my guard down. The killer had sent me one of their grisly trophies, and for what? What message was he trying to send? Did the dismembered body part belong to Illiana Herrera or not?

These questions drilled through my skull as I went through the daily motions at Lou's. The diner buzzed with chatter and laughter around me, a symphony of normalcy that grated on my nerves. Because how could everyone carry on as if nothing had happened? As if this small town wasn't being terrorized by a serial killer who was still on the loose, might I add.

Balancing a tray of steaming coffee mugs in one hand, my eyes darted around the diner at the joyful customers. It was as if the gruesome murders were just a blip in their daily routine, like spilled milk or a traffic jam.

My gaze landed on the group of patrons huddled around the brightly colored flyer pinned on the corkboard near the door. **Town Fair: Fun for All Ages**, it proclaimed—a jolly illustration of a Ferris wheel beneath the bold text. The fair was only a few days away, and that's what held everyone's excitement. The group pointed at the flyer, chattering about cotton candy and funnel cake. Their enthusiasm seemed misplaced, almost grotesque, given the circumstances. Girls were being murdered— dismembered, right here in this very town. And yet, there I was, serving pancakes to people who seemed more concerned with winning stuffed animals than seeing justice brought to the victims.

It made me sick to my stomach. "I can't believe they're still holding the fair," I muttered under my breath while sliding a cup of coffee to a customer.

She glanced up at my comment in disbelief. "Well, aren't you excited about it? I hear the fireworks will be the highlight," she added with a wink.

Shaking my head, I just walked away. I felt trapped in an alternate reality where life carried on, while I drowned in turmoil. All of it drove me mad. The lack of concern and sympathy made me suspicious of everyone at this point.

"Everly—do you need a break?" Lou called to me from a nearby table he was wiping clean.

"I'm fine," I lied, burying my feelings beneath a fake smile.

He grinned, too. "Okay. Could you refill the condiments at table four, then?"

Of course, that's where his concern really lay. I nodded in acknowledgement, going to retrieve mustard and ketchup, all the while wondering if the person squeezing the red sauce could be responsible for the bloodshed that had shaken me to my core.

Like I said, I didn't trust anyone anymore.

My chest tightened, glimpsing my worn-out reflection in the polished silver milkshake machine. Sunken cheeks, dark rings circling my eyes. It was hard to glare at the person staring back at me. She was unrecognizable. But I didn't have time to dwell on my appearance. Sheriff Abernathy's familiar, gravelly voice made my heart hitch into my throat.

What was he doing here? Did he have news for me? Was there finally a breakthrough in the case? Surely, he wouldn't have come here of all places if he didn't have something to share.

I quickly grabbed the condiments and rushed back into the dining area, where Abernathy and Chance sat at the counter, apparently about to have breakfast.

"Order's up!" the cook called, snapping my attention from the officers.

I hurriedly snatched up the plate of grits and eggs for table two—my anger bubbling hotter than that freshly brewed pot of coffee.

How dare they sit there stuffing their faces while Lani's killer was still free?

"Thank you, Everly," the man said at table two as I plopped his plate down with a bit more force than intended.

I wished I could just tilt my head back and scream from the torment of it all. But wait a second—they were in my territory now. Maybe if I got close enough, I could hear what they were discussing—over breakfast.

Whipping out my washcloth, I approached the counter and pretended to clean it, immediately catching Sheriff Abernathy's attention.

"How goes it, Everly?" he asked. But my eyes were on

Chance, whose jaw seemed to clench at the sound of my name. He stared resolutely at his cup, steam curling lazily around his face like tendrils of fog as he pretended not to see me.

So, he was still mad at me then. Figures. I knew I crossed the line by sharing information with Abernathy, despite Chance's discretion. But I was desperate. And it drove me to act impulsively. The sour taste of regret lingered in my mouth as I carefully chose my response to the sheriff.

If I started grilling them about leads, they would probably get up and leave. It was better if I just kept quiet on that front and eavesdropped on what I could.

"Doing my best, Sheriff. And you guys?" I added, hoping to get Chance's attention, but he shifted on his stool, his face turning away from me.

"Can't complain. Lou still has the best BLTs in town," Abernathy said with a laugh, as if everything was all unicorns and rainbows in Graybury.

Biting my tongue, that fake smile returned to my face. "Enjoy," I uttered through clenched teeth. I risked one more glance at Chance, but he refused to look my way. It was frustrating, I admit. The only thing I wanted was answers. Chance, the one person willing to help me, now kept me at arm's length. Because I couldn't keep my word,

I reminded myself.

Swallowing my hurt feelings, I spun and got away from the counter. I abandoned the eavesdropping idea and resumed my duties as if Abernathy and Chance weren't there. My attention remained elsewhere as I bustled around the diner, refilling coffee cups, dropping off plates and keeping the tables clean.

But then, out of the corner of my eye, I saw Sheriff Abernathy excuse himself to the restroom, and Chance sitting at the counter—alone. My heart hammered in my chest as I seized the opportunity. I approached Chance, my clammy hands toying with the end of my apron.

"Hey—" I began, and words trailed off at the exhaustion written all over his face. Apparently, he hadn't slept a wink either. I pushed my glasses off my nose, struggling to figure out how to get answers in the little time before the sheriff returned. My eyes darted to the restroom. Still in the clear, but the clock was ticking. "Can we talk?"

"About what?" His voice was curt, and he still wouldn't meet my gaze.

I sighed. "Chance—come on. I'm sorry I told the sheriff about your investigation…"

"Everly, I trusted you," he snapped, swiveling in his stool to stare at me head on.

"I'm sorry if you got into trouble," I breathed. When our eyes locked, he ran a hand through his thick, coiled hair nervously, his expression softening. I wrung my hands together, hesitantly. "Are there…any leads?"

That time, his eyes flicked to the restroom for the sheriff. "Only that you were right. That finger did indeed belong to Illiana Herrera."

Shocked, I covered my mouth with my hand. Even though I had a feeling it was true, having it confirmed still came as a surprise.

But Chance shook his head. "There's something else you should know," he paused, checking for Sheriff Abernathy again. "Finn is gone."

I staggered back with a heavy gasp. "What are you saying? He's…not in Graybury anymore?"

Chance looked as if it pained him to speak. "I went back to stakeout Finn's place, and he left in the middle of the night. Packed up his things and hasn't been back. He's gone, Everly."

"But Finn did it, Chance. How could you guys just let him get away like that?" I shoved him hard enough to make him come off his stool.

He quickly regained his balance, his eyes shimmering with sympathy. "It's not that simple, Everly. There wasn't any evidence against him. We couldn't force him to—"

"You let a killer go free, Chance. What happened to justice for my sister, huh?" I spun around and stomped away from him with tears prickling my eyes. My chest ached with heavy pain.

How could this be? I practically handed Finn to them, gift wrapped with a bow, and they just let him go. After all the risks I'd taken...

But what if Finn left town because of me? I'd pushed too hard and didn't give the authorities enough time to get tangible evidence, and now Finn was gone. Free to go terrorize another town.

The realization hit me like a punch in the gut. I lured the killer to Lani, and now I'd ruined the opportunity for her killer to be caught.

<hr>

That night, I paced the length of my bedroom, eyes scanning the floorboards as if the answers might materialize from the wood grain. There had to be some way I could make this right. What were we overlooking? How could Finn just slip through the cracks?

Each breath seemed to intensify the pain in my chest. I dug my fingernails deeper into my palms, hoping the physical discomfort would clear my mind. If only Lani were here, she would know exactly where to look and how to navigate this treacherous path. She had tracked this killer long before any of us even knew he existed. Maybe there were clues in her messenger bag.

I snatched it up eagerly and dumped its contents onto my bed. The air felt charged with electric energy as I sifted through the pages, searching for answers. Among the news articles, police reports, and Lani's distinctive handwriting, one folder stood out: Matthias Young. It dawned on me then that I knew very little about the notorious Graybury Slayer case, despite my parents' once constant obsession with catching him. They had always been absent, consumed by their unrelenting pursuit of the deranged killer.

When I flipped open the folder, Matthias Young's mugshot jumped out at me. His cold, predatory stare seemed to follow me as I skimmed through the pages. The stern, older black man's eyes held no trace of humanity, like two bottomless pits.

As I dug through Lani's highlighted notes and police reports, I began piecing together the details of the Graybury Slayer's capture. A break-in had led to his apprehension, thanks to a vigilant deputy who found him with his next victim. DNA evidence linked Matthias Young to hairs found at the crime scenes. No one ever found the trophies.

My eyes scanned over the front page, headlines of

Young's victims:

BEAUTIFUL YOUNG MOM OF TWO, BRUTALLY
SLAIN

MISSING COLLEGE STUDENT FOUND
MURDERED

Each article provided insight into who these women were before having their lives brutally taken away. My throat tightened as I compared these headlines to the small blurbs about the Trophy Killer's crimes—the minuscule columns with grainy images, too tiny to see clearly.

Lani's words proved true. Graybury harbored deep-seated prejudices. The thought devastated me, and I couldn't fathom the struggles of other families forced to rely on a flawed justice system.

As I stared at Young's victims, I realized he had a type—young, white brunettes. And while he took trophies from his victims, they were only belongings, like their clothing and jewelry. The Trophy Killer was far more twisted with his desires. But why minorities? Because he knows the authorities won't do anything? No way was he going to get away with his heinous crimes. Not if I had anything to do with it.

I opened Lani's journal.

Accomplice?? she wrote in one entry.

I flipped to another page dated two weeks ago and read:

BACK FROM THE DEAD??

*After closely recounting the timeline, it appears the
copycat's murders didn't begin until after Matthias
himself died. Almost as if his vengeful ghost Is
back to finish what he started…*

I stared blankly ahead, a shiver crawling down my
spine despite my disbelief in ghosts. It was still unnerving.
The mere thought of someone glorifying these heinous
crimes enough to replicate them made my stomach churn.
What had transpired in Graybury to attract such depraved
individuals from all corners?

I set aside Lani's journals, giving my eyes a much-
needed rest. A throbbing pain bloomed behind them, and
the unanswered questions weighed heavily on my mind.
Collapsing onto my pillow, I squeezed my eyes shut, but
Matthias' mugshot lingered hauntingly in my thoughts.

Suddenly, I popped back up, reaching for the folder

once more. My gaze homed in on Matthias' prisoner number—10462.

Fumbling for my phone, I quickly unlocked it and opened MatchBox, scrolling until I found the profile that'd been taunting me. And there it was, their username: 10462.

NINETEEN

A GENTLE BREEZE PLAYED WITH MY LACE
curtains as I lay sprawled across my bed a few days later, totally drowning in misery. It was a beautiful day for the annual fair, but I was unmoved. Aside from linking the inmate number to the MatchBox profile, I hadn't come up with even a bit of additional evidence against Finn. No wonder they hadn't arrested him yet. It scared me to death that he might just get away with it.

"Everly—" Mom called from the other side of the door. "Are you up?" She stuck her head inside the room.

I groaned, burying my face in my pillow. "No," I grumbled.

"Well, I want you to get up and get ready. We're going to that fair today," she demanded, pausing only to glare at my disheveled appearance.

I propped myself up on my elbows. "Are you serious? The dirt hasn't even settled on Lani's grave and you're thinking about fun?" I couldn't hide my disgust from her.

She sucked in a sharp breath, ignoring my tone. "I know it's hard, Everly, but at some point, we have to move forward."

"Move forward?" I scoffed, plopping back onto the bed. "A stupid fair won't help me move on. I refuse to forget my sister's murder."

"I understand how you feel, Ev. Trust me, I do. But this tragedy can't consume us. Going to the fair doesn't mean we've forgotten Lani; it just means we're trying to find some semblance of normalcy in our lives again."

My eyes stayed on the ceiling, avoiding her. I knew she meant well, but the thought of a crowded, noisy event filled with cheerful people who didn't care that someone murdered my sister infuriated me. Why were they so sure the killer couldn't be out there among them?

I glared at Mom. "But I thought you said to come straight home from the diner."

She placed her hands on her hips, her gaze piercing. "Yes, I did. But we will *not* live in fear, Everly. Besides, the fair will be safe. The sheriff's got a crew patrolling. Deputy Fuller's going to be there, too," she added.

As soon as she mentioned Chance's name, my heart

clenched. Images of his hurt expression at the diner flashed through my mind, and I felt a knot form in my stomach. I couldn't believe I had lashed out at him like that. The dark circles under his eyes were proof of how much this case was weighing on him. And yet, I'd been a horrible friend.

"A couple hours shouldn't be so bad," I said suddenly, pushing myself off the bed.

Mom gave me an approving nod. "I'll meet you outside then."

When she was gone, my stomach churned with anxiety while I slipped into a flowery sundress and stepped into a pair of white sneakers. Every stroke of my hairbrush felt like a betrayal to Lani's memory. But was it, really?

Nobody would want to see me in the mirror pampering myself more than her. I could just hear her teasing me now. It would not satisfy her to see me lying in bed moping on such a gorgeous day.

Mom was right. We had to find some sort of silver lining—a way to keep living while searching for the truth.

The Ferris wheel loomed above us like a watchful eye, keeping guard over the fairgoers below. I'd gone to the fair countless times, but today the cacophony of voices, music, and mechanical noises were overwhelming. But I was not leaving without seeing Chance first. My eyes darted from face to face in search of him. The flashing lights and vibrant colors made me nauseous.

Mom's eyes sparkled with excitement as she looked at me. "I'm happy you're here," she said, nudging my shoulder playfully. My lips tugged into a strained smile, hiding my discomfort.

"I'll go get some food. Want to join me?" she asked.

Where is Chance? my brain shrieked. "Um—no. We can meet back up later if that's okay."

Mom's brow furrowed. "Are you sure you'll be all right? I don't want to overwhelm you."

"I'll be fine," I assured her. "There are cops everywhere, just like you said. I'll stick to the main paths."

Mom still looked uncertain, but she relented with a sigh. "All right. But call me if you need anything."

"I will," I promised.

As soon as Mom disappeared into the crowd, I scanned the fairgrounds again. Somewhere in this sea of people and noise was Chance.

A whirlwind of colors, sounds, and scents enveloped me as I maneuvered through the bustling fairgrounds. Kids zipped by me excitedly, clutching their stuffed animal prizes. Seeing their joy and innocence brought a smile to my face. They were carefree about the ugliness in the world. If I could have that freedom for just five minutes…

Chance came into view, standing at the water gun booth, his khaki police uniform crisp and authoritative.

I wanted to make the most of this opportunity to prove I could be a better friend. So, before approaching, I grabbed a stick of cotton candy, my peace offering. I popped up beside Chance and held out the stick.

"Everly—I didn't expect to see you here," he said, pushing his glasses up on his nose nervously.

I shrugged casually and offered the cotton candy again. He took it with a polite thank you.

"Are you taking a break?" I asked, coming up on my toes anxiously just as Chance stuffed a fluff of candy into his mouth.

He gulped hard. "Yeah—I'm just keeping an eye on things in this area," he gestured to the fairgrounds, his expression falling serious. "And just so you know, we are actively working on your sister's case…"

I positioned myself behind the water gun station, eager to change the subject from a serious conversation. "Race me," I challenged with a smirk.

His brows furrowed in confusion. "Huh?"

"Don't tell me you're scared, Deputy," I taunted playfully.

A slow grin spread across his face as he grabbed the water gun with one hand and even took a bite of cotton candy with the other before aiming at the target.

I couldn't help but roll my eyes at his showboating. "Such a showoff."

With a flick of my wrist, I started filling up my balloon with water. But Chance's aim remained steady, despite his casual nibbling on the sugary treat. He quickly filled his balloon and triggered the alarms for the winner. Of course. It was Chance. As they congratulated him and handed him a stuffed panda, I feigned annoyance.

I playfully elbowed him. "You cheated."

He held the panda out to me. "Peace offering?"

I snatched it and took a bite of his cotton candy, making him laugh. We trudged to the next booth, a bean toss game. The match was already underway.

I smiled faintly. "This was my sister's favorite game."

"I'm sorry she's not here with you. But I promise we're still working on her case," he said again.

I glanced at him, trying to gauge his emotions before cautiously broaching the subject, leaning in close so that our chat remained private. "Doesn't it ever get to you? Being a cop, I mean. Seeing all the things you do. How do you cope?"

Chance was silent for a moment. "It's difficult, that's for sure. But I try to focus on the good I can do, the people I can help. That's what keeps me going."

"I remember how devastated I was when I saw Lani's neck at the funeral. The ligature marks… The funeral director tried his best to cover them up, but—" I shook my head. "It must be so much worse for you, having to see *raw* crime scene photos like that."

A flicker of pain crossed Chance's face, but he nodded. "Yeah, it's—it's difficult. But we signed up for this. I just choose to focus on the positive. For every terrible thing I see, there's a chance to bring someone closure or maybe even save a life." His eyes shifted away from me as he clenched his jaw, the muscles in his face betraying a struggle to maintain composure.

I reached out and lightly grazed his arm, sensing the tautness beneath my touch. "I want to be for you what you've always been for me—a constant support," I reassured him with a warm smile. "Know that you can come to me anytime to talk or let off some steam, too. Seriously," I said with a nudge, trying to lighten the mood.

He looked at me with that guarded expression, but I could see the vulnerability in his eyes. "I appreciate that, Everly."

I turned back to the game. "Round two?"

He slowly grinned. "Bet."

I was grateful that my mom convinced me to come to the fair. Watching families indulge in corn dogs and teenagers laughing on rickety rollercoasters, relishing in the pure happiness of being together, brought a sense of peace. As Lani used to say, life is too short. I wouldn't wish the pain we've gone through on anyone. They should cherish every moment with their loved ones.

Chance and I played a few more rounds of carnival games before he had to return to his duties. As he walked away, I continued to explore the fair, my senses overwhelmed by the enticing smells of frying food and sweet treats. The vibrant booths, adorned with colorful flags and lights, beckoned me closer. The sounds of laughter and joy filled the air, blending with the melodies of cheerful music from nearby rides. Couples strolled hand in hand, their smiles matching the festive atmosphere. Children ran around, shrieking with excitement as they hopped onto one ride after another—it was a lively scene of pure happiness and celebration that swept me in.

When the sun set, I took a break to sit on a bench. I still

clutched the stuffed panda, the reminder of how well things went with Chance. We had a strange connection. We were bound by shared experiences, and although the circumstances were far from ideal, I found solace in knowing we had each other's backs. The sense of ease washing over me was serene. It felt good to let go of the dark cloud looming over me, even if it were for only a few hours.

As I sat, mesmerized by the dazzling lights as nighttime settled, I suddenly heard rustling behind me. When I turned to look, there was no one in sight. But as I leaned back in my seat, a bucket of buttery popcorn appeared beside me with no explanation.

I smiled, glancing around for Chance, but he wasn't there. The surrounding people were too busy with their own activities to pay attention to my presence. So where did the popcorn come from?

Smile fading, I inspected the bucket, the tufts of hair sticking from it—honey blonde hair.

Ice slid through my veins as I snatched the bucket to push aside the popcorn. Lani had dyed her hair. Her roots were dark.

I reached into the bucket and pulled out a handful of strands, causing the popcorn to spill onto the ground. As I brought the long hair up to my eyes, I could see the dark roots clearly at the end.

This was Lani's hair.

TWENTY

 hunched over and my stomach convulsed in agony. Vile chunks spewed from my mouth, splattering onto the ground below. The joyful sounds of laughter and screams seemed distant as the overwhelming sensation of nausea and sickness consumed me.

"Everly!" Mom's voice sliced through the chaos. "Are you okay? What did you eat?" She rushed over and gripped my shoulders.

But I couldn't speak. All I could do was hold out a clump of Lani's hair in my trembling hands, still in shock at what had just happened.

Mom's eyes searched my face with worry as she tried to make sense of the situation. "What—? What is it?"

I blinked at her through teary eyes, my throat burning

as I struggled to answer through heavy gasps. "It's Lani's hair. The killer just left me Lani's hair."

The Ferris wheel cast a kaleidoscope of colors on Mom's frightened face as she backed away, startled, and spun around, jogging ahead, frantically searching for him. "Where is he? Where did he go? Come out, you son of a bitch!" she shrieked, her throat raw.

My legs wobbled beneath me as I struggled to stand and chase after her. The killer was gone, but his presence lingered like a noxious gas. Finn had never left Graybury; he had been hiding all along, waiting for the perfect moment to strike again. And I had foolishly played right into his twisted game.

As if on cue, Sheriff Abernathy stormed onto the scene, drawn by the commotion of Mom's frantic screams. His eyes narrowed with suspicion. "What's going on here?"

"We got another sick trophy, that's what," Mom hissed, pointing back at me and the bucket of popcorn.

"Let me guess—they suspiciously left it for you," Sheriff Abernathy said, glaring at me, but then he flinched as Mom marched toward him, her finger pointing menacingly at his face.

"I do not appreciate your tone, Abernathy. How the hell did you miss this? You're supposed to be keeping this town safe. Why is this killer—"

"Mom. *Mom*." I desperately grabbed her arm, trying to calm her down. "You're screaming," I whispered, glancing at the fair-goers gathering to stare at the scene. Though I understood how she felt, it was still unlike her to lose control.

Her eyes darted around, taking in the prying stares of bystanders. Finally, her shoulders slumped, and she fell silent, her anger replaced by a weary defeat.

Sheriff Abernathy snatched the bucket from me. "Why don't y'all follow me down to the station to talk about this," he said, gesturing for us to come along.

My patience snapped like a twig. All this man did was place us in the seat across from him. When was he going to intimidate actual suspects?

"Mom, we don't have to go anywhere, do we?" I spun to her. "We haven't done anything wrong. Let's just go home."

But she shook her head, whipping out her cell phone. As she thumbed away at her screen, she glanced at me. "Oh, we're going down to the station."

Merely a half hour later, Mom stood outside the sheriff's department, a bank of microphones waiting. Mom's face was a mask of controlled fury as she waited for the signal the cameras were rolling. I stood off to the side among the news reporters, their microphones jostling for position.

Mom took a deep breath before beginning. "As you all know, a series of gruesome murders are plaguing our town, the latest of which took the life of my daughter, Lani Santos."

I shuddered at the mention of my sister's name, flashing back to the horrifying bucket of popcorn. Tears pricked my eyes, but I swiped them away at what Mom said next.

"I will personally oversee this investigation and bring in extra resources from nearby towns to aid us. This killer will not elude us for much longer." She stared directly into the camera with an icy resolve.

"To the monster terrorizing my town, I have a message for you: We will hunt you down. We *will* catch you, and you will *never* see the light of day again."

As the conference ended, Mom stood tall and resolute. Her determination to catch the killer was evident in every inch of her posture. She had successfully prosecuted the Graybury Slayer, and I knew she would do the same with the Trophy Killer. Especially now that he'd made the fatal mistake of targeting someone dear to her, like Lani. This killer was unlike any other in Graybury's history. He took pleasure in taunting the authorities and displaying his twisted trophies. Despite being trapped in his sick game, I had full faith in Mom's ability to bring him to justice.

She waved me over to follow her inside the sheriff's station, where Sheriff Abernathy paced like a raging bull.

"How dare you go behind my back and not discuss this with me?" he bellowed at Mom.

"There's nothing else to discuss," she said icily. "This department has failed to make any progress. And the killer is taunting us, leaving my daughter's hair as a sick trophy."

"We're doing everything we can to catch this guy, Sloane," Abernathy said. "But these things take time."

"Time we don't have!" Mom shouted, fury etching into every line of her face. "This psychopath is getting bolder by the day, and we don't have a single lead. This is unacceptable, Abernathy, and you know it."

He sighed heavily, pinching the bridge of his nose. "What do you suggest we do from here?"

"My contacts at the state level are providing us with experienced detectives and forensics experts. We'll set up a special task force to catch this killer once and for all. I must protect my daughter and put an end to his torment."

"But this is unusual for a serial killer—sending trophies to a civilian," Sheriff Abernathy said. "Normally, they taunt law enforcement, don't you agree?"

"He *is* taunting me if he's taunting my daughter. He's

getting back at me through Everly." She slid her arm around me protectively.

I wanted to tell them they should take a thorough look at Finn, but I kept quiet. If the resources Mom spoke of were coming to help, surely, they would lead to him. And then finally, something would be done.

I couldn't sleep that night. Every time I closed my eyes, images of Lani's hacked off hair plagued my memory. I racked my brain, desperately trying to remember if I saw Finn at the fair. The chaos and noise were too overwhelming to pinpoint anyone, yet somehow the killer found me. How could they have gotten so close without me noticing?

The news of a special task force should have brought some sense of relief, but it only amplified my anxiety. I just wanted this nightmare to end.

My hand hovered over my cell phone, debating whether to reach out to Chance. We had ended things on a playful note at the fair, but then everything went haywire when the killer struck.

As I unlocked my phone, a notification popped up from MatchBox. My stomach dropped as I braced for another message from the Trophy Killer, but it was just an update alert. Curiosity got the best of me, and I opened the app.

Welcome back, Lani2.0. The MatchBox app greeted me cheerfully, as if it had no knowledge of the darkness that unfolded through its connections. My stomach twisted painfully as I remembered the first time I'd signed on, creating the fake profile to get to know a stranger. It'd seemed like a harmless plan in the beginning, but now…

The image of ligature marks on Lani's neck flashed through my mind.

Looking for a new match? The app asked, displaying a slew of potential profiles.

"Wait…" I whispered, sitting up against the headboard, squinting to be sure my eyes weren't playing tricks on me. My blood turned to ice as I stared at a familiar face.

TWENTY-ONE

MY HEART THUDDED IN MY EARS AS I STARED AT the MatchBox profile, clutching my phone with trembling fingers. Gus? This couldn't be right.

I kept telling myself that before the accusations could creep in. But no, it was Gus—my mom's boyfriend—grinning up at me from my screen, familiar crow's feet etched at the corners of his eyes.

The profile was sparse, only a few details filled in. His listed interests included long walks on the beach and candlelit dinners, the sort of clichéd nonsense someone might put if they weren't actually interested in dating. And that's when my alarm bells went off.

I'd always felt MatchBox was the link to everything—that maybe the killer used it to scout victims. Gus, being an attorney, too, would know all the sinister details about Young's case, enough so to implicate his crimes.

Jesus, Everly. I shut my eyes guiltily. A MatchBox profile was proof he was a dirtbag, not a serial killer. But the longer I sat there trying to make sense of it, the more doubt gnawed at my insides, refusing to let me believe anything but the worst.

Gus was a creep; I'd always thought so. And so had Lani. He had practically drooled over her when they first met, his eyes lingering on her body in a way that made my skin crawl.

Ohmigod. I gasped sharply, letting the phone drop on the bed. Did he…?

I scrambled to my feet, unsure what I was about to do. I just felt I should do something.

Going to the police would be pointless. They'd just ask what proof I had besides my gut feeling. And if I'm wrong about Gus, I'd be risking my mom's relationship.

Oh, no. Poor Mom. My heart sank at the thought of hurting her. Regardless of the outcome, this news would devastate her.

That's why I needed solid proof before telling anyone. But how? Did I need to go back to the Herreras with a photo of Gus?

No way. They were going through enough. Plus, they already confirmed Illiana didn't use MatchBox. Although, she fit Gus's type—young and pretty. Where else could they have met?

Exhausted from my thoughts, I crawled into bed, my mind consumed by the chaos.

The next morning, I sat at the table, picking at a bowl of cereal, racking my brain to make sense of that profile. What if Finn was using a picture of Gus to throw me off track? But that profile never contacted me. MatchBox just might be Gus's tool to cheat on my mom. And while it was shady in my book, it meant nothing to the authorities.

I let my spoon clink against the bowl, the cereal soggy as it floated in the milk. Lani was right about our taste in men.

"Everly, you look so blue," Mom said, strolling by me to pour herself a cup of coffee. "We are going to catch this guy, okay?" She placed a hand on my shoulder gingerly. I nodded, silently praying that the guy they caught wasn't her boyfriend. She pulled away from me at the sound of a car honking out front. "Must be Gus," she murmured.

"Gus?" I echoed.

"Mm-hmm. We're carpooling this morning." She gathered her things and headed for the front door, missing the panic in my face. "Text me if you need anything," she called. As the front door shut behind her, I zipped out into the backyard to hop on my bike. I needed to be quick if I wanted to catch up with them.

A flickering neon sign cast an eerie glow on the sleazy motel. My heart pounded so loudly in my chest I thought Gus could hear it as he climbed out of his car. I stooped lower behind the row of overgrown bushes, out of sight.

After he dropped Mom off, I trailed Gus here, desperate to know what he was up to when Mom wasn't around. Whistling casually, Gus strolled up the steps to Room 56. And sure enough, a few minutes later, a woman arrived and knocked on the door.

My breath caught in my throat. That woman certainly wasn't my mom. She was young and attractive, with a cascade of dark curls. As she disappeared inside Gus's room, I sank into the grass, defeated. What was I to do now? Call the police or leave it alone? What if this woman was the next target? I didn't get a good look at her to know if she fit the killer's type.

"Hey—what are you doing down there?" a voice called out from behind me.

I jumped, stifling a scream. Turning, I found an older man in a janitor jumpsuit eying me suspiciously. "Just fixing my bike," I lied, pretending to fumble with the tire.

The man narrowed his eyes. "Uh-huh, well, you can't loiter here. Get going," he snapped, jabbing his thumb in the opposite direction.

I nodded, hurriedly climbing onto my bike, and pedaling a safe distance further, all the while keeping my eyes on Room 56.

What was happening inside that room? If I didn't do something, and that woman ended up dead... I could never live with myself. I fumbled for my phone in my pocket. Hands trembling, my thumb hovered over the dial keys, preparing to call the police.

To tell them what? That Gus was guilty of cheating on my mom?

How long was I going to dance to this tune? Calling the police with no evidence. I glanced wearily at the door of Room 56. I wasn't sure how much time had passed, but eventually the door opened, and the attractive woman emerged. There wasn't a hint of distress on her face, only satisfaction. Gus appeared beside her, and they shared a passionate kiss that twisted my stomach into a pretzel. The thought of Gus betraying Mom like this disgusted me, but I was relieved the woman was okay.

Having seen enough of that, I got as far away from the motel as possible. But my business with Gus was far from over.

"What's up?" Chance asked, stepping out into the parking lot after I'd texted him to meet me outside the station. I didn't want to go inside and risk Mom seeing me and becoming suspicious of my plan.

"Hey, thanks for coming out," I said, totally stalling before getting to the point. He nodded, waiting for me to go on. "Um—I have a favor to ask." I wrung my hands together, bringing my voice to a whisper so only Chance could hear. "Could you run a check on Gus Dearborn—off the record?"

His eyes bulged. "Your mom's boyfriend? Why?"

"I just followed…" My words trailed off as Chance's face fell.

"Everly, we've been through this," he said, his tone disappointed.

"I know, but the guy's a creep. I just caught him messing around on my mom."

Chance uttered a shaky breath in surprise. "That's really effed up," he murmured, running a hand through his coiled hair nervously. "But why am I checking him out? You think he is a suspect because of this?"

I shrugged. Telling him about the MatchBox profiled seemed far too petty of a reason to investigate Gus. "If he's capable of this, who knows what his background looks like? I have to protect my mom," I added. That made

Chance agree with me.

"Okay—I'll let you know what I find out, but Everly, please, go home."

<hr>

I'd been sitting in my room that night when I heard the front door slam, followed by some angry stomping up the stairs.

"Everly—?" Mom's voice clipped, just before barging into my room. "Have you lost your mind?" She stood in the doorway and planted her hands on her hips.

My shoulders sagged. Of course she'd find out. I just didn't expect her to so quickly. And I'm pretty sure I got Chance into trouble. Again.

Mom looked at me with wide, bewildered eyes and uttered one name. "Gus?" She threw her hands into the air.

I hesitated, torn between telling her the truth and protecting her feelings. "Mom, I'm sorry, but…"

"Everly, this has got to stop. I know you want someone to blame, but this is getting out of control."

"He's cheating on you," I said flatly, Gus's secret rendezvous replaying in my head like a twisted movie reel.

She lowered her hands, her expression never wavering.

"How do you know that?"

"I saw him today, meeting a woman at a motel." I didn't need to say anything more.

My mom's reaction was as if I punched her in the gut. Blinking rapidly, her lips pressed into a tight line. But her intense gaze returned almost immediately.

"I've told you before, Everly, no more juvenile sleuthing. It's not safe," she said, changing the subject. I tried to read her expression, but it remained guarded.

She pointed a finger at me. "I'll have you locked in a holding cell if that's what it takes to keep you safe. Don't think for a moment I won't." She turned abruptly and left the room.

Words couldn't explain the guilt I felt having to tell her the truth about her boyfriend, especially with everything else she had on her plate already. But what did Chance find out?

I snatched my cell to shoot him a text. He was probably still fuming at me, which I couldn't blame him for, but I needed to know if Gus was up to anything more than just fooling around. As I typed, erased, and retyped how to address Chance, my phone pinged with a notification from MatchBox. It was from 10462.

I gripped my phone anxiously, eager to know what he had to say. He hadn't texted me for some time now.

I opened the text and met with nothing more than an address.

> **10462:** 736 Sycamore St

TWENTY-TWO

MY PALMS WERE CLAMMY AS I CREPT DOWN THE stairs. After spending an eternity trying to decipher what the cryptic address could mean, I decided to find out. I had raced through the connections since the investigation began and nothing linked to that address. Neither serial killer nor their victims. It was even in the opposite direction of Finn's lake house.

I knew going to the address could be playing right into the killer's hands, but the idea of discovering something crucial to the case was too tempting to ignore. So, I texted the address to Chance and asked him to meet me there. Of course, he told me to stay put, that he would check it out on his own. But the killer wanted me to find something, and I wanted to know what. That's why I slipped out the back door, avoiding the watchful eye of the officer stationed out front.

As I hopped on my bike and pedaled through the dark, empty streets, I tried to silence the nagging inner voice questioning my sanity.

What if this was a trap? What if the killer was there waiting to murder me next? Or…what if another victim needed my help? Like a race against time to save their life or something.

Pedaling furiously, the night air whipped against me as if trying to hold me back. The deserted streets seemed to stretch on forever, but finally the dilapidated house came into view. I braked in the overgrown driveway and peered at the house.

Silent. Dark. Menacing. The isolated Victorian structure loomed ominously against the moonlit sky. Its shattered windows left gaping holes that seemed to stare back at me, daring me to enter. It was like a decaying monster hidden within the shadows.

What awaited me on the other side of that door? A heavy feeling of dread settled over my body, as Chance's warning echoed in my mind—stay put. But I continued to climb off my bike, attempting to shake the chill slithering down my spine. There was no way I could just sit idly by while the secrets of this house remained unknown.

I crouched behind a rotting fence to survey the surroundings. The abandoned location had no neighbors, no traffic, not even the sound of crickets filled the air. It was as if the world had ceased to exist beyond this forsaken spot. Yet the killer brought me here for a reason. What did he want me to find?

My eyes fixed on the dark windows for any hint of movement. Perhaps he was waiting at one, rifle in hand, ready to take my head off. But that wasn't his MO. He preferred a more intimate approach to murder, up close and personal.

Okay, Everly—let's just see what's inside. Taking a deep breath, I mustered up all my courage and crept toward the front door. The gravel and debris crunching under my shoes flushed my stealthy approach down the toilet. When I finally reached the door, I hesitated, wondering if I should wait for Chance. But the urgency of discovering what was on the other side propelled me forward. I gripped the cold doorknob, and turned it slowly.

The darkness inside the house swallowed me whole, leaving me momentarily disoriented. A musty odor greeted my nostrils, and I fought the urge to gag. The atmosphere felt thick with a malevolent energy that raised the hairs on my arms. Every fiber of my being screamed for me to turn and leave, but there were answers here. I could feel it.

Moonlight seeped through the cracked windows,

casting eerie shadows on the decaying walls. A floorboard creaked beneath my foot, and it seemed to echo throughout the house. Or at least I thought it did. I stood frozen, ears straining for any sign I alerted someone.

Silence.

I didn't know what I was searching for, but if I didn't find it in the next couple of minutes, I was hightailing it out of there. That was if the smell didn't kill me first. The air was so stale and extremely putrid that my skin crawled with revulsion. What caused that awful stench?

Fumbling around in my pocket, I grabbed my phone to use its flashlight. As the beam of light pierced the gloom, it revealed peeling wallpaper and dusty furniture—remnants of a life long forgotten.

With a hand over my nose and mouth, I forced my legs to inch forward. The silence was so deafening that my breathing sounded like thunder in my ears. The flashlight flickered across an open doorway, and suddenly, I felt someone—or something—lurking in the shadows, watching my every move.

"Hello?" I croaked, my voice barely audible. Instantly, my fear morphed into anger at myself for being so reckless. It was clear no good could come from this place. And yet, there I was. So, I might as well see it through. Without hesitation, I barged into the next room and something cold and stiff brushed across my face. I staggered backward, the flashlight trembling violently in my hand as the beam illuminated the source of the chilling touch.

A human foot. Blue jeans. T-shirt.

The scream that tore from my throat was raw and primal.

A disfigured corpse dangled from the ceiling, its lifeless eyes staring blankly into the void. Screaming again, I spun around and crashed into someone else. Familiar cologne wafted over me, and gentle hands clutched my shoulders.

"Whoa, it's just me," Chance cried. I collapsed into his embrace. I needed to tell him about the body, but my sobs choked back any words that tried to escape. "Okay—okay, let's get back outside, all right?" Chance said.

Nodding, I allowed him to lead me away. Even outside in the fresh night air, I still felt the lingering touch of cold, lifeless skin against my own. The smell of death seemed to cling to me, refusing to leave my senses. The reality of what had just happened engulfed me, and panic rose like bile in my throat. I thought I was going to be sick. My breaths came out shallow and ragged.

"Everly," Chance called, cupping my face gently, forcing me to meet his gaze. "Just take deep breaths, okay, remember?" He stared into my eyes sincerely.

I nodded vigorously, taking in shaky breaths of air. Afterward, I clutched onto his arm as he guided me to his truck and onto the passenger seat.

"Wait here. I'm going to call the sheriff to help investigate this," Chance said, shutting the door, but I caught his wrist.

"Chance, I swear," I choked out, eyes watering all over again. "I didn't know what was inside. I didn't know."

He carefully pried my hand from his arm. "I'll be right back." He shut the door and went off to make the call.

I tried to read his expression to see if he believed me, but I couldn't tell. They couldn't possibly think I had something to do with this, did they?

Oh, god, no. My hands covered my face as I plopped against the seat, focusing on my breathing, desperately attempting to calm my racing heart. Why would the Trophy Killer send me here? More importantly, who was that hanging? Another victim?

Mind reeling with questions and fears, I stared blankly out the windshield until the sound of crunching gravel snapped me out of my panicked reverie. Sheriff Abernathy's cruiser came to a halt behind the truck, and Mom pulled up beside him.

"Mom," I whispered, turning in my seat for a better view. In the dim light, I saw her step out of her car with a purposeful stride, her icy eyes scanning the scene as if ready to dissect every detail.

Chance met her and the sheriff halfway. I watched as they exchanged tense words. Mom shot me a glare, her expression softening at the fear on my face. Chance told them what he knew so far—which wasn't much—each of them glancing at me worriedly.

As Mom and the sheriff entered the house, Chance hung back with me—his presence a minor comfort amidst the chaos. But within moments, Mom emerged from the house, eyes wide in fright, with Abernathy right on her trail. Their voices, at first muffled, grew louder and more intense.

Why was Mom so upset? Did she know the victim? I shakily climbed out of the truck, just as she put both hands to her face in despair. "Mom, what is it?" I was almost too afraid to ask.

She turned to me, her face pale—her tough exterior cracked. "That's… Arthur—Arthur Frye," she said, her voice heavy with the weight of the realization. "Jeffrey's ex-partner."

My heart pounded in my chest as the implications set in. Arthur? But why? Why would the killer send me to his dead body? I didn't know Arthur at all.

"Shit," Mom hissed under her breath. "He's coming for

me," she muttered. Her eyes met mine, and she looked as if she'd forgotten all about me. "Oh my god, Everly." She spun to Chance. "Take her home so she can pack a bag."

"Mom?" I cried.

"Everly, not a word. You're going to Wood River with your dad until we catch this psycho."

"Wait a minute, Sloane," Sheriff Abernathy interjected, crossing his arms.

"No!" Mom exploded. "Can't you see? He's hunting everyone involved in catching Matthias Young." She growled in frustration. "Son of a bitch!" She whipped around on me. "We have to get you out of Graybury until it's safe."

Sheriff Abernathy stepped closer, his hawk-like eyes scrutinizing. "I'm sorry, Sloane, but we can't just send Everly away."

"Excuse me," she snapped, turning to face the sheriff with blazing eyes. "It's my duty to protect my daughter…"

"Your daughter could be the key to catching this killer," the sheriff argued.

I blinked between them both, unsure whose side to take. While I wanted to get as far away from Graybury as possible, I wanted nothing more than to see this monster caught.

"I hope to god you're not suggesting using my daughter

as bait because you can't do your job," Mom hissed, jabbing the air inches from the sheriff's face.

"How does Everly know of this place?" he demanded.

Mom shifted as everyone's eyes fell on me.

Wringing my hands together, I gulped. "The killer sometimes texts me on MatchBox…" My voice was small. A hush fell over them as they absorbed my words. Then Mom blew up.

"Why wouldn't you tell us this?"

"Because you wouldn't have believed it. I still think the guy is Finn, and look how that turned out," I said, staring pointedly at the sheriff.

He just shook his head. "Again, if you send Everly away, we might lose our best chance at catching this guy. He seems to have a connection with her," he said, throwing his hands into the air as if he were all out of options.

Mom took a deep breath, her eyes narrowing with determination. "Then we will take over the MatchBox account if that's the key to reaching him," she said firmly. "And instead of wasting any more time on Everly, we need to set up a perimeter around this crime scene and find evidence. And get somebody to get Arthur off that goddamn rope," she shouted, her voice breaking on the end, her eyes tearing up. I forgot she and Arthur had history. That poor man. He sacrificed everything in pursuit of a murderer, only to succumb to the hands of someone even more sadistic.

I reached out to console Mom, but she pulled away, gathered herself, and firmly held out her hand. "Phone…"

I knew that wasn't up for discussion, so I handed my cell over. Hopefully, they could trace him somehow.

Mom turned to Chance, her tone authoritative. "Take her to Wood River. Now."

Chance gave a curt nod. "Let's go, Everly."

I took Mom's hand first. "Please be careful," I told her quietly.

She threw her arms around me in a quick embrace. "This will all be over soon," she promised. Though her voice was confident, her eyes told another story. She was fearful. But I believed in her. She was strong and driven. If anybody could solve this, it'd be her.

I kept telling myself that as Chance and I climbed into his truck. But as we left the scene, I felt there was no escaping this killer's twisted game. What if nowhere was safe? Surely, if he sent me to Arthur's body, he would know my dad lives in Wood River. No matter where I went, he was watching, waiting for the perfect moment to strike.

TWENTY-THREE

RAIN—ONCE AGAIN. THAT'S ALL IT SEEMED TO do in Wood River was rain. The drops fell like a thousand tiny silver daggers, piercing the evening gloom that enveloped the small town. It mirrored my mood as I stared out the bedroom window of Dad's trailer home, feeling like a prisoner. My heart ached for updates about the case, but everyone was giving me the cold shoulder. I was in isolation—this ten-by-ten-bedroom the solid proof.

That wasn't fair. Dad had been nothing but a good sport the past few days, going above and beyond to make my stay worthwhile. We had a movie marathon, visited local landmarks, and even spent a night playing cards and eating pizza. It most likely was just his attempt to make up for lost time. But I couldn't fully enjoy any of it. My mind remained anchored in Graybury, consumed by the unsolved case. Why would the killer lead me to Arthur's corpse? Was it suicide or murder?

So many questions with no answers…

My eyes wandered to the burner phone Dad gave me, since my phone was now evidence. The more I thought about it, the angrier I got. Because the Trophy Killer kept reaching out to me for a reason. And I would never know why. Being miles away from Graybury in this backwater town did nothing except push me further from the truth. At least back at home, I felt like I was helping. Here, all I could do was sit and wait and wonder.

Shifting to the edge of the bed, I gripped the edge of the mattress tightly, hoping to force the image of Arthur's hanging corpse from my memory.

"Ev, dinner's ready," Dad called. Almost immediately, the smell of garlic and olive oil wafted through the air, probably from a full course meal.

Sighing, I pushed myself off the bed to go join him at the table. As I took my seat, he slid the plate of food in front of me.

"You have pan seared salmon, buttery garlic green beans, and roasted rosemary potatoes," he said. "Do you like sweet tea? I brewed it fresh yesterday."

I felt like I was in a five-star restaurant. Everything smelled delicious, but it did little to lift my spirits. "Um, no, I'm okay."

With a shrug, he turned back to the stove to make his plate, whistling and dancing to his own tune. He was overly cheery whenever he was around me. It was as if he was trying to compensate for something, to make me forget the grim reality we lived in. But when he thought I wasn't looking, I'd seen him on the phone, angry and irritated. This was bothering him, too. Arthur was his ex-partner—he must've been feeling something over his death.

The silence hung heavy in the air as we ate. Dad had made such an effort to make this meal, I didn't want to just push it back and forth on my plate. Yet if he really wanted to satisfy me, he could answer my questions about Graybury instead of keeping me in the dark.

He gestured toward the ring Lani gave me. "That's a pretty cool ring you have there," he remarked. My fingers instinctively curled around it as I remembered the purpose behind its design—self-defense.

"I was thinking," he said between chewing, "once all this rain lets up, we could go fishing. There's this lake..." he went on, speaking animatedly about his latest fishing trip as if we had a normal life. "...you should have seen the size of it. It was unreal!"

My gaze lingered to the kitchen window at the

raindrops racing down the glass. Just like the race against time to catch this killer.

"...and you don't care," Dad said, leaning into my view.

"I'm sorry, Dad. I'm just thinking about Graybury. Have you heard anything more about Arthur Frye?" Surely, he wanted to know what happened to him, too.

"Everly," Dad paused, his gaze softening as he regarded me, the cheeriness in his voice wavering. "You're supposed to be enjoying your time with me, not obsessing over that case."

I knew he was trying to protect me, but the thought of a killer still on the loose—potentially watching my every move—was a constant thorn in my side. Wood River might have been peaceful and idyllic, but it couldn't keep me from the truth.

I stabbed a potato with my fork. "We both know I didn't come here for a vacation," I grumbled.

"But you're safe here and that's all that matters."

"What matters is why the killer wanted me to have his trophies," I snapped, letting my utensil clank onto my plate. "Why did I have to find Arthur's body?"

"Honey, please, let the authorities handle it. They will catch him and then we can all finally move on with our lives." He shoved a fork full of food into his mouth, dismissing the conversation.

My lips parted to ask to be excused when the shrill ring of his cell phone interrupted. My pulse quickened at the sight of Mom's name flashing across the screen. Was she calling with an update?

Dad scooped the phone up quickly. "Excuse me," he said, sliding back in his seat. He didn't take the call until he was in the next room, out of earshot.

I strained my ears to hear the conversation, but all I could make out were snippets of his tense, muffled voice. Another argument.

Suddenly, my phone buzzed. It was Chance. Perfect timing. "Did you guys find the killer?" I asked when I picked up.

"Hello to you, too, Everly. Trust me, you will be the first to know once that happens. But no, we have not caught him yet." His voice faltered in the end.

I pushed my food back and forth on the plate as the conversation dried up. "Well, it was nice of you to call."

He was quiet for a beat, and I could just picture him running a hand through his thick hair as he searched for words. Finally, he said, "I'm sorry. I know how much this means to you, how much you want to help. But it's Sloane's orders not to keep you involved." He paused to swallow. "I just wanted to check in on you and make sure you're doing okay. When you found that body…"

I shut my eyes, chills running through me at the icy touch of death brushing against my skin that night. "Can you at least tell me if there have been any more victims?"

"No, there haven't. Arthur Frye is the latest."

"So, the Trophy Killer murdered Arthur?"

"Yes."

"But why? And why stage his body to appear as a suicide?"

"That's what we're busy figuring out."

"Well, how did he die?"

He sighed. "It was good to hear from you, Everly, but I must get going now. Take care of yourself, okay?" The line went dead.

I stared at the phone as if that would bring him back. Anger crept into my bones. They weren't being fair to me at all. If not for me, they wouldn't have even found Arthur, yet I didn't have the right to know what happened to him. I slammed the phone on the table just as Dad returned.

"Who were you talking to?" he asked.

"No one," I muttered, struggling to swallow another bite of food. I couldn't help but notice the change in my dad's demeanor. Irritation replaced his usual cheeriness. "What happened?" I asked, looking at him expectantly.

He took a sip of his tea, attempting to mask his actual feelings. "What do you mean?"

"That was Mom—is she all right?"

"Oh, you know your mother," he muttered, taking a bite of food. I tried to recall a time my parents were together when they weren't fighting. It seemed they were only at peace when they were apart. But now I'd practically forced them back into each other's lives.

"Are you guys fighting about me?" I demanded, forcing him to meet my gaze.

His eyes softened as he reached across the table to place a hand on top of mine. "Honey, no. It's just…" He drew back. "Sloane has so much on her plate right now. Losing Lani…this psycho murderer…and now she's broken up with her boyfriend."

I gasped, having forgotten all about Gus. How could Mom focus on anything while suffering from so much heartache?

"Her only solace is your safety," Dad said, interrupting my thoughts.

My gaze snapped to him upon the realization of the nuisance I must've been to her throughout this entire investigation. The last thing I wanted was to burden her. Yet, that's all I'd done so far when I reflected on my actions—the many calls to the station in the middle of the night. I'd made her life a living hell. But this was all the killer's fault. Why did he have to choose us?

<hr>

"What will it be, Ev?" I heard Dad asking, but my eyes darted around the ice cream parlor, searching for any sign of danger. "Honey?" He placed a hand on my shoulder, jolting me from my trance. "Why don't you go snag us a table while I order, yeah?"

Swallowing, I nodded and spun on my heel and tried to focus on the parlor, the colorful posters on the wall of ice cream cones with cherries and sprinkles. I settled in a booth in the back where I could see out the window and see the front door at the same time. In the beginning, I'd thought leaving Graybury would bring some semblance of peace, but I felt even more on edge. The killer was out there somewhere. And just because they took my phone away didn't mean he wouldn't find me.

Immediately, my eyes peered out the window again, scanning the street for anything unusual. I glanced around nervously, half-expecting to see the shadowy figure of the serial killer lurking behind every lamppost.

Wood River was picturesque, with historic brick

buildings and tree-lined sidewalks. It may have seemed safe, but until they caught the Trophy Killer, I would never feel safe anywhere.

"Ta-da…" Dad appeared, two towering sundaes in hand.

I forced a smile, knowing full well I didn't have the appetite for that. But seeing the hopeful look in his eyes, I dug in and scooped up a spoonful that tasted like ashes in my mouth. "Yum," I uttered, forcing another smile.

Dad slid into the booth beside me and devoured a spoonful of his sundae.

My stomach churned as I poked at the hot fudge, thinking of blood and hair and severed fingers.

Stop it, I told myself. Nothing can happen in this sweet little ice cream shoppe.

Something shattered. A child screamed. I let my spoon go as I jumped in my seat, searching for the killer.

Dad slid an arm around me protectively. "Sweetheart, relax," he whispered, giving me a tight squeeze. "You're safe here, I promise."

I wanted to believe his assurances, but the gnawing fear that the killer was still out there refused to let me.

Dad studied me with a cop's assessing gaze. "Listen, kiddo, I'm sorry you're going through what you're going through, but you only get to be sixteen once. I know it's hard, but for as long as you're here with me, I want you to focus on being a teenager. No more obsessing over Graybury and serial killers or anything else grim, okay?" He took a scoop of ice cream and flew it like an airplane to my lips as if I were an infant.

Smiling, I opened my mouth wide and took a big bite. "Deal." As we polished off our sundaes, we made small talk about plans for tomorrow, when his buzzing cell phone shattered the fragile bubble of happiness we'd just created. I watched as his face transformed from amusement to concern as he read the text. The tension building in his jaw was a sure sign that whatever news he was receiving wasn't good.

"Everything okay?" I asked, my voice small. Part of me wanted to know if it was an update on the Trophy Killer, but I didn't dare ask. I wouldn't get the truth, anyway.

He sighed heavily. "Sorry, sweetheart, but it looks like duty calls. They need me at the station, but hey—" He placed a hand gingerly on my cheek, staring me into my eyes. "I'm going to have Deputy Collins sit with you until I get back. It should take me less than thirty minutes." He kissed me on the forehead before sliding out of the booth. "Gotta run to the bathroom really quick."

"Okay, Dad." As he slinked to the restroom, I couldn't even be upset that work called. For the past few days, Dad had made me his priority, given me his undivided attention. And I appreciated him for that.

"Here ya go," a young boy's voice interrupted my thoughts. I looked up to see a small, freckled face staring back at me. He was maybe nine or ten. The boy held out his hand, presenting me with a disk. "Someone told me to give this to you."

"Me?" I choked out, completely taken aback by the intrusion. "Who?"

He shrugged. "Well, I don't know. They just said to give it to you." He set the disk on the table and skipped away nonchalantly, slipping out the door.

Panic creeping in, I glanced around the parlor again. Who sent me this?

I inspected the disk, noticing the words scrawled against its surface. **PLAY ME**

My heart leaped into my throat as I recognized the squiggly handwriting. It was the same as on the package containing the sawed-off finger.

TWENTY-FOUR

SWEAT DRIPPED DOWN MY FOREHEAD AS I SAT IN front of Dad's computer, the blank screen reflecting my own uncertain expression. I couldn't bring myself to obey the PLAY ME command written on the disk. Instead, my hand shook uncontrollably, hovering over the mouse pad with every fiber of my being screaming for me to just play it already. This was undoubtedly a message from the Trophy Killer, and the unknown contents filled me with a sickening anticipation. What horrors awaited me? Would it reveal another victim, their tortured cries reverberating through the speakers? Or something worse, like a recording of Lani's brutal homicide? The mere thought caused a lump to form in my throat, and I couldn't bring myself to click on the file.

It was a cruel twist of fate. I had been praying for any

lead, any hint that could tell me the killer's next move. And now that I had this piece of evidence in front of me, all I wanted was to throw it away and pretend it didn't exist. The killer had mockingly left me his macabre trophies—a finger sawed off from one victim, strands of my sister's hair, and the location of another body. What would be his sick game this time? Would I have to watch Lani's last moments before he brutally took her life?

My head hung low, a heavy ache weighing on my chest. Tears blurred my vision as I cautiously peered through the curtain, searching for any signs of Deputy Collins's cruiser. It sat ominously at the curb, its windows dark and foreboding.

A sense of solace washed over me, knowing he was there, keeping watch. And soon enough, Dad would be back, too. Maybe I should just hand the disk over to him and never find out what secrets it held. But then it hit me—the Trophy Killer had it delivered to me for a reason. There was something he wanted me to know.

Despite my inner turmoil, I pressed play.

The screen flickered and illuminated the room in a blue glow before the video began. Dread and anticipation seeped through my veins as the video started.

"Chaos unfolds today as we stand outside the residence of Annie Young, the sister of Matthias Young, the notorious Graybury Slayer," a news reporter spoke, her voice distorted by the passage of time. The camera panned to show a swarm of angry protestors lined outside Annie's modest house, the front yard littered with garbage.

"Get out now! Get out now!" The protestors were chanting, waving signs with images of Young's victims printed on them.

Annie stood in front of her house, staring the protestors down. The news reporter thrust a microphone into Annie's face. "I am not my brother!" she shouted, the veins in her neck straining with every word. She was middle-aged with brown skin and low cropped dark hair speckled with gray. Her dark eyes flashed in fury as she gestured to the mess on her lawn. "Look at this!" she said to the reporter. "I can't take this anymore. They vandalize my home every day with spray paint, busted out windows and trash. It's not right."

"Then leave!" a protestor rang out.

"Matthias was not me!" Annie shouted back in frustration, desperate to make them understand. "I am *not* responsible for what he did."

I slid to the edge of my seat, my pulse quickening with every heated exchange between Annie and the protestors. The air I breathed suddenly felt thick with tension and unresolved anger. Annie's pain drew me in. True, the protestors were seeking justice for the victims, but in their quest for vengeance, they were creating a new victim.

"As long as a Young continues to live in our neighborhood, our families will never be at peace!" someone shouted.

Annie shook her head tirelessly, tears forming in her eyes. "Enough is enough. It's not just me who is suffering," she told the reporter. "My son is just a child. He's innocent of all this, and yet he's being bullied and harassed. This isn't right," she said, her voice cracking.

The protestors started chanting again, their voices a cacophony of hate against Annie's resolve.

She turned to the reporter helplessly. "You see? Nothing's being done to stop this. I've tried calling the sheriff out here, but he doesn't care about us. We've done nothing wrong. Where's our justice?"

"Now, Ms. Young," the reporter interjected, her tone cold and unfeeling, "let's not forget who the actual victims are here—the six innocent young women *your* brother savagely slaughtered. Don't you think staying in this neighborhood is opening a fresh wound to their loved ones?" She thrust the microphone back into Annie's face again, who choked on her words.

Just then, the screen door creaked open behind her, revealing the face of a young boy peering from the darkness. "Mom?"

"No, baby, stay inside," Annie warned, her voice sharp with maternal instinct. She turned back to the reporter, face hardened and jaw set. "I have nothing more to say." With that, she turned her back on the chaos. As she took slow, deliberate steps to her door, the camera panned to focus on her retreating figure.

I gasped, my eyes widening as they locked onto the small glimpse of the boy standing behind the screen door. My hands shook as I hit the rewind button, managing to freeze the frame just in time. The boy's image locked on the screen, his eyes—familiar eyes—staring straight into my soul.

My hand flew to my mouth as I slid back in the seat, a sickening moan slipping from my lips. "God, no."

TWENTY-FIVE

MY MOUTH HUNG OPEN AS I STARED AT THE frozen image of a young Benjamin. His wide-eyed innocence captured in the frame did little to hide the horrible truth. Benjamin was the Trophy Killer.

I shook my head in denial, even as my mind raced to process this bombshell. It couldn't be true. Not prim and proper, Benjamin. But there was no denying the evidence before me. "How?" The word croaked from my bone-dry throat.

"The real question is *why*, Everly," Benjamin's velvety voice answered from behind me.

I jolted from my seat, startled by his sudden appearance. My heart pounded as I stared into the abyss of Benjamin's cold eyes. He stood, prowled in the doorway, clad in all black—black pants and a black hoodie with the hood pulled up over his head.

How did he get inside the house? My eyes flitted to the curtains, attempting to peer out for Deputy Collins, but Benjamin's next words shattered all hope.

"Oh, no, he won't be coming," he said, casually flicking something onto the desk beside me. A small metal rectangle gleamed under the computer screen's glow. A name tag reading **DEPUTY COLLINS.**

The twisted grin on Benjamin's face made my skin crawl, and I fought the urge not to scream. I couldn't give him a reason to hurt me, not yet. Not until Dad came back. Swallowing hard, I forced myself to meet his stony gaze. "That news report…" I managed to point toward the screen behind me without breaking eye contact. "That should never have happened to you and your mom. You two didn't deserve to be vilified—you were innocent."

A flicker of emotion passed through his eyes, a fleeting glimmer of vulnerability, before the darkness once again consumed them. He stared at the image of his younger self, frozen on the screen.

"Just days after that, they burned our house to the ground. We barely escaped with our lives." His voice was icy. Bitterness seeped through every word. "We lost everything—our belongings, our identities…" He placed a hand over his chest, as if trying to contain an overwhelming pain.

I nodded, feeling sympathy for the destruction he had to endure at such a young age. "I'm so sorry that happened to you."

"Pity is meaningless, Everly," he snapped, taking a slow, deliberate step closer.

My body went rigid as my brain scrambled for another way to reach him. "Is that why you became this, the Trophy Killer?" I asked tentatively, hating myself for giving him a reason to justify his actions. But I was desperate to keep him talking—to keep his focus on my words instead of the murderous instincts I saw simmering just beneath the surface.

I longed for any sign of the gentle guy who used to make me feel safe, but he was gone. In his place stood a sinister figure, radiating danger and menace.

His eyes bored into mine, a storm brewing inside them, a tempest of rage and betrayal. "That was just the beginning, Everly."

"Talk to me then, Ben. Help me understand why you did this."

He blinked at me with eerie calmness. "You've always been one for solving mysteries. Yet, you still haven't pieced this one together."

I glanced back at the screen. "You're right. You've been leaving me breadcrumbs, but I'm still slow to understand.

So, tell me."

A heavy silence hung between us, suffocating like a leaden shroud. Benjamin's intense gaze bored into me, his lips pressed into a thin line. I felt the weight of his words before he even spoke them.

Finally, in a soft voice filled with pain, he said, "Your parents are part of a festering problem in this town, Everly."

My stomach twisted at the accusation. "What does my family have to do with anything? You mean capturing your uncle?"

"Your parents," he spat, each word laced with venom, "destroyed my life. Matthias was guilty of robbing that woman, but he didn't kill anybody."

My heart pounded thunderously as my brain raced to make sense of his claims. "Are you saying that they captured the wrong man?"

Benjamin's eyes burned into mine. "I'm saying Sloane and Jeffrey *framed* Matthias. They knew he was innocent."

The air seemed to seep out of me as I drowned in my own frantic thoughts. Was that true? Could my parents really have played a part in such a monstrous injustice?

"No—they couldn't have known Matthias was innocent," I uttered, shaking my head in disbelief. "They—couldn't have…"

But Benjamin's icy stare never wavered. "The real Graybury Slayer was Arthur Frye. Your father discovered Arthur was the murderer and instead of arresting him, Jeffrey and Sloane framed Matthias."

The room spun as I tried to find some rationale, some explanation that would absolve my parents from such a heinous act. "But why? There has to be more to it than that. There must be some mistake," I croaked, tears pricking my eyes.

"Everly, there's no mistake," he said coldly, his gaze unwavering. "They pinned the murders on Matthias because it was easier to ruin the life of a black man than a sadistic cop. Sloane made the town feel safe through vilifying my family."

As his words slapped me in the face, I felt trapped in a nightmare I couldn't escape from. The walls seemed to close in around me, suffocating me with the weight of buried secrets and whispered lies. And although I wanted desperately to believe in my parents' innocence, a tiny, insidious voice inside my head kept whispering that maybe—just maybe—Benjamin was right. The story Dad told about Arthur drinking and losing his job. Was that a lie? And Dad's moving to Wood River. Was that because he couldn't face what they'd done?

"No—*no*—" That's all I could muster, unable to find

the words to express my hurt and confusion.

Benjamin's eyes blazed with anger as he charged toward me, his muscular arm gripping my shirt and slamming me against the wall. My back hit the icy surface with a thud, the impact knocking the breath out of me. He towered over me, his features twisted in a dangerous scowl.

"I don't care what you or that fucked up town believes," he growled, reaching into his hoodie to retrieve a USB drive hanging around his neck. "I have the proof right here," he continued, releasing my shirt to clamp a powerful hand around my face. His grip tightened so fiercely I felt the blood vessels pulsing under his fingertips.

"This is Arthur's confession. And I am going to clear my uncle's name once and for all, but not before sending everyone involved in his injustice straight to hell." His vice-like grip slammed my head against the wall in rage.

A jagged bolt of panic shot through me, every muscle in my body tensing. Thrusting my fist forward, I aimed the self-defense ring directly at Benjamin's face. A cry of pain tore from his throat as the tiny dagger found its mark in his eye, blood spurting from the wound like a crimson fountain. Benjamin staggered back, clutching his face, and howling like a madman.

Instinct took over, and in a split second, I snatched the

USB drive from around his neck and bolted from the room. I slammed the office door shut behind me and threw my weight against the door while fumbling with the lock. My fingers were slick with sweat, but I managed to turn the lock just as Benjamin's body collided with the door from the other side.

"Everly!" he roared monstrously.

Tears blurred my vision as I sprinted down the narrow hallway to my bedroom, but a deafening crash echoed through the house and sent chills down my spine. Shattered glass tinkled, and I knew with dread Benjamin had escaped.

TWENTY-SIX

THE CAR RADIO CRACKLED AS YET ANOTHER news reporter droned on about the connection between Matthias and Benjamin. With a swift movement, I jabbed at the power button, silencing the irritating voice. I couldn't stand to hear any more of the twisted half-truths that made their way into the media.

They apprehended Benjamin the morning following the break-in. Authorities discovered a blood trail that led them straight to his hideout in a neighbor's shed, where he'd blacked out from his injuries. It should have been a triumphant moment, but all I felt was a gnawing sense of injustice.

Benjamin's capture satisfied Graybury. In their eyes, it was finally over. But I couldn't help wondering if things would ever truly come to an end, or if the shadows of the past would continue to haunt my family.

My chest tightened with an overwhelming sense of guilt. Guilt for what my parents did to Matthias. Guilt for my own mistakes and hasty judgment with Finn. I longed to find him and make amends, but he had disappeared without a trace, leaving me with only remorse. And Deputy Collins… Authorities discovered his crumpled body in the trunk of his car. And it was all my fault. If only he hadn't been trying to protect me, Benjamin wouldn't have murdered him.

I stared out the window, annoyance simmering in my gut. The trees slid by in a blur of orange—early signs of fall. It was funny how life just moved on.

"Everly," Mom said, her voice cutting through my haze of thoughts. "I understand you're angry, but we need to talk about this. Your bitterness isn't helping anyone. You hardly spoke a word at the ceremony today." She took her eyes off the road briefly to glance at me.

The thought of Sheriff Abernathy's boisterous celebration for the arrest of the Trophy Killer made my stomach turn. Despite their efforts to honor me with a toast, only Mom and I knew the truth about Benjamin's actions. The air was thick with false praise and misguided admiration as people clinked glasses and raised their voices in cheer. But I couldn't bring myself to join in on the façade. It all felt like a cheap carnival act, masking the dark reality of what my parents did.

"Ev," Mom began, cutting herself off with a desperate sigh.

"Clearing Matthias Young's name is necessary, and you know it," I seethed. Angry tears pooled in my eyes at the reminder of Arthur's confession on that drive. Though he was bound, bruised, and beaten into submission by Benjamin, Arthur recounted in chilling detail the lives he had stolen—the pain and terror he'd inflicted on innocent young women. He'd even given the location where he'd kept his trophies. Even after all those years, he still had them.

I'd given Mom the USB drive with the hope she would set the record straight. Yet, so far, nothing has been done.

She shifted, squeezing the steering wheel tighter as we wound down a curvy road. "Your heart is in the right place, Everly, but you need to understand that the world doesn't always work the way we want it to." She cut an eye at me, voice softening. "It's a messy, complicated place, and sometimes, we have to pick our battles for the sake of maintaining order."

"Meaning?"

"Meaning…that for now, we are going to get through Benjamin's trial before presenting further evidence about the Graybury Slayer. My goal right now is to bring justice to Benjamin's victims. Afterwards, I promise you we will make everything else right."

No. That wasn't enough for me. Shaking my head, I spun to her, unable to contain myself. "Matthias died in prison, Mom—for a crime he didn't commit. Graybury is still talking about him like he was the monster when really…" I cut myself off, attempting to get a hold of myself. My entire body was shaking. "Why haven't you spoken about the USB drive yet?" I demanded.

"Everly," she hissed, swerving the car to an abrupt stop. "That coerced confession would not have held up in court. The only thing that drive is good for is connecting Arthur to the trophies he kept on his family's farm. Once Benjamin's trial is over, then will we use that information to clear Matthias Young's name."

I clenched my fist, willing myself not to snap back with the question that'd been haunting me for days. I didn't need to ask; Mom already knew what I wanted to say.

"Listen," she said firmly, turning to face me. Though her eyes were full of sorrow and regret, she kept her chin strong, her posture straight. "I know you don't understand why things happened the way they did, but I need you to trust me when I say that it wasn't easy for me to make those choices."

Scoffing, I turned away from her and folded my arms

across my chest. My jaw clenched as I struggled to contain the anger bubbling within me. "Choices?" I spat out bitterly. "You speak as if deciding between apples and oranges at the grocery store. Your *choices* destroyed an innocent man's life. And look where it has led us."

She snatched my arm, forcing me to face her. "And I have to carry the weight of that every single day, Everly," she snapped, her voice cracking with emotion. "But sometimes, you have to do what's necessary to survive in this world. Being a woman in law enforcement wasn't a walk in the park," she confessed, her eyes glistening with unshed tears. "I fought tooth and nail to get where I am today, and sometimes, that meant making decisions I wasn't proud of. Decisions that kept me in the game, and ultimately gave me the power to shape the course of justice." She looked away, shame etching lines in her face. "I did what I had to do to claw my way to the top. It's not something I'm proud of, but it got me to a place where my voice matters."

My heartbeat thundered in my ears as I stared at her, wanting to rage and scream and condemn her and Dad both for their moral failings.

"I promise you, Everly, that I will make this right." Blinking back tears, she held her hand out to me. After a beat, I slid my hand inside hers, and though relief washed over her face, I struggled to reconcile my love for her with the rage burning inside me.

———————

When we got home, the pile of mail met us on the floor. I collected it, sifting through bills and junk letters, and froze when I spotted the crisp white envelope addressed to me. The return address—Iron Valley Penitentiary. The letter was from Benjamin.

"Anything for me?" Mom asked, brushing by me to dump her keys on the table.

I stuffed the envelope into my jacket pocket, pulse racing. "Uh, yeah, just this." I handed her the stack. "I'm gonna go get changed," I said, quickly dashing up the staircase.

"All right, but come back—I'm ordering take out," Mom said.

"Okay," I called over my shoulder. Once inside my room, I shut the door and leaned against it as I shakily tore the envelope open.

Come see me

That's all the letter said.

I gazed at the words, feeling a surge of nausea in my

throat. He actually wanted to see me. The thought of being pulled back into his twisted world made my blood boil. How could he have the audacity to disrupt my life and then demand my presence whenever he pleased?

I crumpled the paper and hurled it in the trash. My mind reeling, I started pacing and chewing my nails to the quick.

Why did he want to see me? Did it even matter? Benjamin was right where he belonged, locked away so he couldn't hurt anyone else. And yet, he was still reaching out to me. Why couldn't he just leave me alone?

While pacing the length of my room, every few seconds glancing at the crumpled ball in the trash, my resolve hardened. I still had questions and no answers. Maybe this was an opportunity—a chance to confront Benjamin and get those answers.

I grabbed my phone and texted Chance.

Up for a road trip?

The afternoon sun cast long shadows across the dusty road as Chance's truck rumbled to a stop in front of the imposing jailhouse the next day. The building loomed before us, its weathered bricks and bars giving it an air of dark history. I stared at the structure, my pulse quickening in anticipation.

"Everly…" Chance began. His voice was low and filled with concern as he turned off the engine. He pushed his glasses off his nose, his wide eyes searching for understanding.

My own nerves were on edge as I swallowed hard, feeling the weight of his worry. Despite supporting my decision to see Benjamin, Chance's concern grew as we made the three-hour drive. And now that we were here, it was evident in every line of his face.

"I know you feel you must do this but be careful. This guy is a monster. He's gonna try to get into your head. Just remember, you don't owe him anything."

I knew Chance was right, but he wasn't aware of the secrets between Benjamin and my family. Not telling him the truth was painful. It felt like I was perpetuating my parents' web of deceit, as if I was silently accepting their actions and their wrongdoings. But I clung to the hope that they would eventually do what was just and fair. Right now, I needed answers from Benjamin.

"I can go with you, you know…" Chance offered, tracing circles on the steering wheel with his finger nervously.

"That's sweet of you, but I don't think Benjamin would

be as honest with a cop sitting there," I said gently. While I meant that, I really couldn't risk Chance overhearing anything Benjamin, and I were going to talk about.

I took Chance's hand. "Thank you for always being there for me. I don't know how I would've come this far without you."

He glanced away shyly. "It's my duty to help, Everly. I'll be right out here if you need me." He squeezed my hand.

The familiar warmth of his presence enveloped me like a cozy blanket, soothing my worries and filling me with a sense of security. But that all disappeared the moment I climbed out of the truck and went inside the jailhouse. Despite Chance's words, a tiny part of me believed I owed Benjamin something because of what my parents did to his family. Had they not framed Matthias, none of this would've happened.

Yet, my sister and the other victims didn't deserve what happened to them, either.

My footsteps echoed through the empty space, punctuated by the distant clangs and shouts from within. This was the belly of the beast, a place where nightmares were born, and yet it held the key to my salvation.

A uniformed guard checked my identification and escorted me to a seat in the visitation area where Benjamin was already waiting on the other side of the glass. The black eye patch he wore was a stark reminder of the damage Lani's ring had done.

I took a deep breath before picking up the adjacent phone. For a moment, we sat in silence, his one eye locked on me.

"I'm here," I said finally, steeling myself for whatever was to come, refusing to look away from his piercing stare.

His voice cracked gruffly into the receiver. "What did you do with that USB drive?"

The USB drive? That's why he wanted to see me? No. No way.

I shook my head, my voice quivering with rage. "No, you answer me. Why did you torment me with your twisted messages and sick trophies? Why me?"

A cruel smirk played across his face. "I thought you were better than your parents, Everly. I believed you would use the knowledge I gave you for good, but now I see that was a mistake." His words dripped with malice. "Now, *where* is that drive?"

My breaths came out sharp. "You have the nerve to talk about good after all the pain you caused. Those girls you killed were innocent. How could you target minorities?"

"Everly…" He shook his head in disappointment. "Even after everything, you still don't understand. Choosing them was necessary. A means to an end." He leaned back smugly in his chair, almost relishing the way I furrowed my brow, trying to decipher his words.

"What end?"

Sighing, he shifted the phone to his other ear. "Graybury is rotten to its very core, Everly. Its justice system only favors pretty white victims. The girls I chose were sacrifices," he said, his one eye never leaving mine. "Sacrifices to expose the ugly truth about this town. The truth," he repeated, a slow grin spreading across his face. "The truth is more dangerous than the lies, Everly."

I broke his gaze for a beat, gulping hard to force down the knot in my throat. My heart pounded in my chest with a sickening mixture of fury and sorrow. "You chose to become a monster, Benjamin. You're deluded if you seriously believe what you did was right."

"Whether my actions were justified or not, they exposed the true nature of Graybury to you. Can you honestly deny that your perception of this town has changed since then?"

I bit my lip, fighting back tears. It was gut wrenching to agree with him, but I couldn't deny the truth in his words. Graybury was a cesspool of racism and injustice, but that shouldn't justify the horrors he committed.

Swiping my eyes dry, I straightened my spine. "You're no better than Arthur Frye. No one deserved what you did. You murdered and mutilated innocent girls. My sister—" The words died on my lips as my eyes pooled all over again.

"Lani… Poor Lani," he whispered her name. "I really did like her, you know. She was—"

A bitter, acidic sensation rose in my throat as I pulled the phone away from my ear. I couldn't stomach listening to him talk about her. My eyes shut as I remembered Chance's warning.

He's gonna try to get in your head.

I couldn't let that happen. Taking a slow and steady breath, I opened my eyes. Benjamin's forehead pressed against the glass as he motioned for me to come closer with a finger.

Slowly, I put the phone back to my ear and wished more than anything that I hadn't.

TWENTY-SEVEN

AS I SHUT THE DOOR, MOM'S VOICE ECHOED through the house. "Ev—I'm in the den!"

It was well past sunset when Chance and I finally returned from our journey to the jailhouse. Seeing Benjamin had, both mentally and emotionally, taken its toll on me. Despite the warmth of the house, a chill still ran through me, aching my bones. I wrapped my arms around myself, trying to rub away the goosebumps dotting my skin. The fall air outside was crisp and unforgiving.

Making my way to the den, I found Mom on the couch, a crystal glass of red wine cradled in her hands. Her once bright blue eyes were now sunken and tired, but they lit up as soon as they met mine. "Come sit with me," she said, patting the spot next to her on the couch. "I made us a fire."

My shivering body eagerly complied with her request as I dashed over and nestled into the cushions next to her. The crackle of the fireplace provided a comforting backdrop to our conversation.

With a contented sigh, Mom slid her arm around me, pulling me closer. I couldn't help but inhale deeply, taking in the familiar scent of her lavender perfume. "You know," she began, her voice soft and wistful, "when Lani was just becoming a teenager, I used to let her celebrate my wins with me and have a glass of champagne." A fond smile tugged at the corners of her lips as she reminisced. "It made her feel so mature."

A small smile spread across my face too as memories of my older sister flooded back—moments filled with laughter and shared secrets. "I miss her," I admitted softly.

"Oh, I miss her, too. I regret not telling her how proud I was of her. I'm proud of you, too," she said, holding me closer. "Both of you possess my drive and determination. It makes me feel like I've done well," she boasted, having a sip from her glass.

"True," I said with a nod. "Lani was on her way. If only she had the chance to expose Arthur's crimes…"

"Oh, yes," Mom agreed. "That would've been her lucky break…"

"Mom," I whispered, pulling away from her, "is that

why you killed her?" I stared into her eyes, seeing the pain and loss reflected there. But also, something else—something darker.

Time seemed to stop as we stared at each other, locked in a battle of wills. Not even the crackle and popping of the fire could break our gaze.

I licked my dry lips, finding my voice. "Benjamin says he didn't kill Lani. He copied the Graybury Slayer and only murdered six girls, too. And when I think about it, I realized the only person who wouldn't want the truth about Arthur to get out was you."

Mom just sat there, staring into the fire as if it held the answers she couldn't give me. Her knuckles were white as she gripped her wineglass so tightly it seemed on the verge of shattering. The flames danced in her pooling eyes.

"Mom please," I choked, desperate for some kind of denial, an explanation that made sense. "Tell me I'm wrong."

She took a shaky breath, her voice barely audible when she finally spoke. "Everly, I loved your sister more than anything. You know that."

"Yes, I know. But what happened?"

She swiped away a tear trailing her face and sniffled. "Lani and I—we were arguing, as usual. She kept asking me these questions..." she shut her eyes, shaking her head, "so many questions about Arthur—didn't think his disappearance added up." She sucked in another breath, swaying as if she might faint. "Somehow, she figured out the truth, and she was furious at me. Accused me of protecting him, of putting my career ahead of everything—even you." She looked at me, her lips quivering. "I never meant for things to escalate the way they did… I just—I snapped." She tried to grab my hand, but I snatched away. "Everly, I am so sorry, honey, please…"

"Just stop," I whispered fiercely, my voice trembling as I got to my feet. "You didn't just strangle Lani to death, Mom. You shaved her head to make it look like the killer did it. Then you *left* her hair for me to find. Ohmigod!" I backed away, chest heaving. "You are never clearing Matthias' name, are you?" I shouted, lowering to the floor helplessly. The realization of my mother's true nature literally tore me to bits.

Sobbing, I peered up at her disgustedly. "Of course, you won't do the right thing. I was stupid to trust you."

"Everly—" she rose to console me.

"Don't you dare come near me!" I swatted her hand away, trembling with anger and betrayal. "Lani was right about you. You are selfish and don't care about anything except for your precious career."

My mother's face twisted into a sneer as she glared down at me, her eyes flashing with defiance. She towered over me as if trying to intimidate me into silence. "Sloane Baker is Graybury's savior," she hissed through clenched teeth. "Once I convict Benjamin, they will hail me another hero. And absolutely no one is gonna take that from me, especially not you." She jabbed a finger at me.

"Oh, we'll just see about that," I sneered, hurrying to get to my feet. "Chance—you can come in now."

Mom's eyes bulged as Chance entered the living room.

After piecing together the truth at the jailhouse, I revealed everything to Chance during our tense ride back home. I even handed him my copy of Arthur's confession. If anyone could do what was right with that footage, it would be Chance.

That's why I sneakily let him inside the house to eavesdrop on our confrontation. I'd hoped beyond hope that I was wrong about my mother. That maybe Benjamin had been lying to me, trying to turn me against her. But no… She had committed the ultimate betrayal.

Despite the shock written all over his face, Chance maintained a professional composure as he presented a pair of gleaming silver handcuffs to my mother. His voice held a hint of sadness as he began reciting Mom her Miranda rights, slowly approaching her with caution.

"Sloane Baker, you are under arrest for the murder of Lani Santos…"

Mom's eyes pleaded with me, searching for any sign of mercy or forgiveness. Her voice strained with emotion as she struggled against Chance's firm grasp, her arms clasped behind her back.

"Please, I'm not a bad person. I am your mother, Everly."

The desperation in her gaze was suffocating as she begged for my understanding. But I couldn't bear to listen to her pleas any longer. I turned my back on her without a word.

"Everly, no matter what you may think of me, I will always be your mother," she snapped. "Nothing can ever change that."

I whirled to face her, tears streaming down my face as I glared at her with seething rage. "You're wrong. You stopped being my mother the moment you killed my sister." I put a hand over my mouth to muffle the sob that tore from my throat. "Chance, please…just get her away from me."

He nodded solemnly, tugging Mom toward the door.

"Everly, no. Everly!" she continued to scream my name as Chance escorted her from the house.

GO GRAB YOUR FREE BOOKS

When you subscribe to my mailing list, you'll instantly get *The Perfect Daughter* and *The Perfect Ride*. Plus, you'll be the first to know about my new releases, special offers, and other fun stuff. (Rest assured, I will *not* flood your inbox. ☺) Visit **nikikeith.com** to get your download.

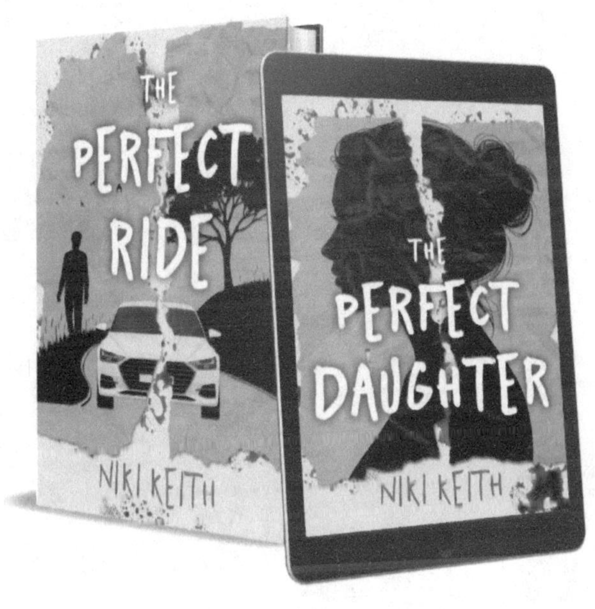

1

EDDIE

NOW

I silently vowed that I wouldn't knock out Riley's teeth.

"Here we are," Diego declared, rolling his shitty Charger to a stop.

Wes, my twin brother, glanced at me from the passenger seat and picked up on my grim expression. "Oh, lighten up, bro. It's only two days," he said as he pushed the door open.

I hurried after him. "So, did we really have to invite *him*?" I muttered, eyeing Riley leaning on his outdated station wagon—just one look at his handsome features and killer smile made me cringe.

Diego came over and back-slapped me hard on the chest. "We're here to patch things up. Now quit bitching and grab your stuff."

I didn't even flinch. My eyes locked on his as my

knuckles itched to knock some sense into his boyish face. I could do without his bullshit, too.

He chuckled and spat a glob on the ground. Disgusting ass pig.

"You heard the man," Wes said, bumping shoulders with me.

It was typical of him to side with Diego—sometimes you'd think *they* were brothers. Fuck it. The sooner I got this over with, the sooner I'd be away from them. I grabbed my backpack and tossed one to Wes. A couple of cases of beer sat beside Diego's duffel bag, just what we needed to set the official weekend from hell in motion.

My eyes flicked to the abandoned cabin Wes and I had discovered when we were thirteen. It was supposed to be our secret—until his loyalty to Diego took over.

Brooklyn's BMW purred up the rocky trail behind Riley, vibrating with muffled pop music. My heart skipped a beat. She would definitely make the weekend worthwhile. I suppressed my grin; if anyone cracked a wisecrack, I'd be scratching that knuckle itch.

Brooklyn's best friend, April, hopped out of the passenger seat in sunglasses, her denim short shorts revealing her toned dark-brown legs and a tube top that barely covered her boobs. The guys craned their necks to take it in.

But not me—I only had eyes for Brooklyn, who sat

hesitantly behind the wheel. She, too, didn't want to be around Riley. None of us wanted a party, especially after what we had done. Our lives would be over if anyone ever found out.

My gaze met Brooklyn's. She gave a small wave; I returned a curt nod. Maybe we could sneak away and camp somewhere apart from the others. That was the plan—to use the cabin for our personal stuff and camp out because it was unbearably hot. It wasn't as if the place had much to offer—it didn't even have electricity, though our LED lights and lanterns made up for it.

For Wes and me, having the cabin meant a private sanctuary to escape from Hank. God knew our dad wasn't exactly Father-of-the-Year. Lately, we'd been using the cabin for everything but a haven, though.

"Good—all our besties are here," April said overly cheerily.

Riley knew damn well he no longer had that title with me. Any of us, really. He'd burned us, and I wasn't about to pretend it hadn't happened.

April held up two bottles of vodka. "What do you say we get this party started?"

Wes lunged forward to grab one. "Now, I'm all in for that—a shot party!"

"Uh-uh. You can get the food out of the back," she

snapped, clutching the bottle close to her chest, out of his reach.

Wes scoffed and headed for the cabin. "Like hell I will," he muttered.

Riley, still leaning against the station wagon, laughed. "Can we just get this thing going already? I'll help with your stuff since *I'm* the only gentleman here," he said, flashing a toothy grin.

I clenched my fist. Let Riley be, Eddie.

April fluttered her thick, false lashes at him as if he had angel wings. "Aww, thank you, Riley."

I'd had enough. Clutching my bag, I followed Wes up to the lopsided porch. The slate-gray log cabin featured a family room, a half bathroom with working water (miraculously), and an attic-sized bedroom upstairs that Brooklyn and I claimed since we were the only real couple in the group. Wes and April were on-and-off lovers.

The hot, musty living room came complete with a loveseat, coffee table, and oriental rug courtesy of Brooklyn. A fireplace burned fiercely in the winter when lit properly. The back wall held built-in shelves with a set of cast iron skillets left by the previous owner. We kept them, unsure if we'd ever actually cook our meals on them.

Sandwiches and roasted marshmallows made up the menu for the day.

"Why don't we do this?" Diego suggested, unable to

resist his inner control freak. "Let's split into groups. Wes, Riley, and I can set up camp. April and Eddie can gather what we need for the fire. And Brooklyn can prep the food. There—we're all doing our part."

"Me and *April?*" I spun around and glared at Diego.

"I'm pretty sure they'd have to come looking for you if you're with Brooklyn," Diego replied with an eye roll. "Besides, it's only a few hours until sundown. We've already wasted enough time."

Brooklyn appeared, handing out juices. "I'm fine with prep duty," she said with a shrug and a small smile in my direction.

"Oh, come *on* already," April insisted, shoving the vodka into Brooklyn's hand. "Don't worry—I'll bring your boyfriend back in one piece."

"Creepy, isn't it?" April remarked, nearly an hour later.

"What?" I grumbled, swatting away a low branch that barred my path. The heavy, humid air had me sweating profusely. Who in their right mind thought camping was a good idea, anyway?

"It's the isolation. We're completely alone. No one's around for miles," April replied, her eyes shining with excitement.

I smacked a mosquito on my arm. "I'd say it's more annoying than creepy." I shot a glance at Diego and Wes, impressed by their work. They had managed to set up one tent and were strutting around as if it were the Statue of Liberty. I couldn't fathom why Wes was so enthusiastic about the trip. We'd agreed to limit our time with Riley to avoid more drama. Regardless, we were all here—the whole gang.

I bent down to clear a thick branch when a piercing scream sent me sprawling face-first into the dirt.

April laughed. "Told you it's creepy. Diego, you owe me twenty bucks," she said as Diego and Wes approached.

I hauled myself up, my shirt and shorts now filthy and my palms caked in mud. "You're an idiot," I muttered, wiping my hands on my shorts.

April wrinkled her nose at me. "Did you really think I was being murdered?"

Wes snickered. "If you were, no one would hear your screams from miles away."

"That isn't funny," I snapped.

"Aww—why don't you crawl back to the cabin and cry to your girlfriend about it?" Diego taunted.

I narrowed my eyes at him. "At least I have a girlfriend. You're just a third wheel," I added under my breath.

April's jaw dropped.

Diego stepped forward, his jaw clenching. "What the

hell did you just say to me?"

"Whoa," Wes interjected as he leaped between us, one hand on each of our shoulders. "Seriously, just go chill in the cabin, man. And tell Riley to get his ass back here."

I kept my eyes on Diego a moment longer before glancing at Wes. "Why isn't Riley with you guys?"

Wes rolled his eyes. "Typical Riley bullshit. He complained of a stomachache and left to get some water. That was thirty minutes ago."

Lazy fucker. I veered away, ducking over a log as I tried to navigate back to the clearing. "Yeah. I'll go get Riley."

Riley. Everything was his fault. Well, not entirely—the events of last Halloween had a lot to do with it—but Riley was the final straw.

The cabin soon emerged into view, and I hurried over, thinking it was the perfect moment to mention to Brooklyn that we should try camping somewhere else. Instead, inside the cabin, nothing but four blank walls stared back at me. On the table lay bread and condiments, untouched.

"Brook?" I called softly as I ascended the creaky stairs. The cracked bathroom door hinted that no one was inside, yet I still peeked in. Nothing. I moved towards a closed bedroom door, about to knock, when the voices behind it made me pause. Brooklyn and Riley were together in there.

I held my breath and listened.

"Riley… wait… I don't…" Brooklyn's voice trembled with panic.

"No, you can't back out on me now. Come *here*."

Brooklyn shrieked.

My heart pounded against my ribcage. I twisted the doorknob, but it refused to open. "Brooklyn!" I pounded on the wood with my fist.

She gasped. "Eddie?"

I tugged harder. "Open the goddamn door!"

Brooklyn screamed, "Let go of me, Riley. Stop!"

I rammed my shoulder against the door repeatedly. "Riley, you piece of shit." Eventually, the old wood splintered and the door burst open. Riley had Brooklyn pinned against the wall with his forearm as he clumsily fumbled with the button of her jeans. "Get off her!" I shouted, grabbing his shoulders and wrenching him around. He staggered, desperately trying to keep his balance, his eyes wild and sweat pouring down his face. What the hell was wrong with him?

I shoved him hard. "What the hell are you doing?"

A sloppy grin spread across his face as he swayed. "Go back outside, bro." He turned again to Brooklyn, roughly seizing a handful of her hair.

"Riley—stop!" I clutched his shoulders, hoping to pry him away from Brooklyn, but he only pulled her along with him.

"Fuck off!" He elbowed me. "Brooklyn said this was okay."

"What?" Her voice became shrill.

My vision blurred, and I punched Riley square in the jaw. As he staggered and swung at me, I dipped, driving my shoulder into his waist and knocking the wind out of him. Riley grunted and gasped for air, falling backward with his hands outstretched for support.

I lunged with my arm extended, but his ivory fingertips clawed at air. It was too late. Glass shattered. Riley shrieked—and then he was gone. Brooklyn and I rushed to the broken window and watched in horror as Riley fell to the ground below.

Brooklyn screamed, trembling with shock.

"Oh, God… I didn't…" The prickling fear along my neck stole my words. A gust of wind slithered through the shattered window, sending a chill down my spine. It was as if I were caught in a whirlpool: everything spun, morphing into grotesque shapes I could barely recognize.

Then Riley came into focus below, sprawled on a cluster of jagged stones. I stared at him, willing him to move. I pulled myself away from the broken pane, glass crunching beneath my sneakers. Small drops of blood gleamed on my shaking hands. "Brooklyn…" I whispered hoarsely.

She turned away, sobbing silently. I bolted down the stairs.

"What the hell was th—" Wes nearly collided with me as I surged out the front door.

"It's Riley!" I called, darting from the porch and skidding to a stop at the edge of the rock pile. Riley lay flat on his back, his arms splayed, blood trickling onto the stones. The image seared into my mind as I stood frozen in time. A bird screeched from a nearby tree, jolting me from my trance. "Riley?" I hardly recognized the high-pitched sound of my own voice.

Wes brushed past me to investigate while I hung back. He carefully crawled over the rocks and reached for Riley's neck, then turned to me with a horrified expression. "Holy shit, Eddie… Riley… he's dead."

2

EDDIE

NOW

"I have no idea where Riley could be, Coach Donahue," I said, the words scorching my throat as I gripped the phone so tightly I almost crushed it. The Donahues—Riley's parents—didn't begin calling until Monday evening, two days after Riley had disappeared.

Coach Donahue cleared his throat. "Are you sure, Edward? I know how Riley can be. If he said something to you, I promise I won't be upset. His mother's car is gone, too. I—" he sighed, "—*we* just want him to come home.

I swallowed hard to keep my throat from closing. "Um, I'm certain, Coach. I haven't heard from Riley since Friday night—at Mario's birthday party. If he calls, I'll tell him to phone home." I ended the call and exhaled in a long whoosh, like air escaping an overinflated balloon. Tears stung behind my eyes as I clutched the warm dryer, trying to pull myself together, groaning at the churn in my stomach. I already felt hollow from days of vomiting. I took a deep breath—in and out, in and out. By the third round, my shoulders relaxed and the tightness in my chest eased. Slowly, I opened my eyes. Alright. Back to work.

I reached inside the dryer for the warm, rainforest-scented bundle when I noticed an olive-green shirt that had appeared out of nowhere. My heart rate surged—where the hell had that come from? I dropped the load and prodded the green top as if it were alive. It was Mom's shirt, of course; olive green was her favorite color. Yet Mom had left nearly eleven years ago. So why was it in the laundry? I shook my head and tossed it in the trash. It had to be Hank's doing. Our father, Henry Hawkins—better known as Hank—swore he'd kill us if we ever called him dad. But Wes and I had a different nickname for him: Monster.

After finishing folding the laundry, I quietly made my way up the basement steps, removing the key from around my neck. It belonged to Mom and opened the double-locked knob on the basement door, her refuge. Wes and I each had matching copies, much to Hank's annoyance whenever we locked ourselves in there. He could have changed the lock, but he refused to invest in the crumbling house. The place clung on by a thread, and people assumed it was vacant. The shutters banged against the siding even in the softest breeze, and there was no telling what lurked in the knee-deep grass. I supposed it was partly my fault—whenever Hank got drunk, he'd yell at me to mow the lawn, only to forget about it once he sobered up. I knew yard work, but honestly, I didn't know where to start.

The sick, yellow tint in the hall reminded me of an old hospital room, and a truck commercial blared from the ancient floor-model TV in the den. Creeping into the kitchen, I spotted Hank's shiny brown head in the busted La-Z-Boy, his nine-millimeter pistol resting on the end table. For some reason, he always kept his gun within arm's reach—perhaps as a reminder of his hay-day as a cop.

Hank tilted his bald head back and downed the final swig of his Budweiser. I was grateful he wasn't drinking something stronger. Why the hell was I spying on him, anyway? I cautiously stepped away from the doorway; we had to be careful around Hank's paranoia. Wes had barged in on him before, and Hank had turned and shot at him—the bullet hole in the kitchen wall was a grim reminder.

"Come here, Eddie," Hank suddenly barked, startling me. Did he have eyes in the back of his head? I dropped the laundry basket near the doorway and approached his chair. "What're you staring at?" he demanded, eyes fixed ahead. "I can see your damn reflection."

Right. "I was just passing by," I said, trying to sound casual. Not that Hank would ever notice when something was off—Wes hadn't been home since Friday, and Hank hadn't caught on yet. Finally, he turned to me, eyeing me with disgust. "Well, pass by the fridge and bring me another beer."

I nodded and began to step away when a news broadcast stopped me cold. "—a local jogger discovered the body this afternoon—" the newswoman announced. I stared at the TV while everything around me seemed to move in slow motion, the reporter's words fading into slurred, indistinct sounds. "—authorities are yet to release further details—" I gulped hard. What did she mean? A body found where? I nearly screamed. Could it be Riley?

"Dumbass." Hank's face loomed as he leaned over the arm of his seat. "Go fetch my beer before someone finds *your* battered body, and bring me a bowl of chips, will ya?"

I made my way to the kitchen on unsteady legs, clutching the counter to steady myself. Just breathe. It couldn't be Riley, could it? That night we'd been so sure that—

I fished my cell from my pocket. I had to reach Wes. But when I called, his number rang once before going straight to voicemail. "Of course," I muttered, hanging up.

"Edward, if I have to come in there..." Hank said,

jostling me into action.

I searched every cabinet, finding nothing suitable—Hank hadn't picked up groceries in ages, let alone a bag of chips. Instead, I found a pack of saltine crackers in the cupboard that would have to do. With another beer, Hank probably wouldn't notice the difference anyway. But my mind kept returning to that mysterious body—I had to get a hold of Wes.

I grabbed another Budweiser and returned to the den, straining to catch the words on the blaring news discussing scattered thunderstorms for the night. Holding the beer and crackers out to Hank, I said, "Here."

"What the hell is that?" he growled, his glare shifting from the pack of crackers to my face.

"It's all we have." My eyes landed on the pistol. Was it loaded? I didn't want to risk finding out.

Hank snatched the items from me and slumped back into his seat, shoving two crackers into his mouth simultaneously. "Don't just stand there watching me. Make yourself useful and change the goddamn channel."

Hank liked to boast about being a boxer back in his day, which was hard to believe given his current state. I glared at the crumbs on his belly; he was such a slob. As I dragged myself toward the TV, something whooshed past my head, hit the wall, and shattered into pieces—it was his empty beer bottle.

"Move your ass." Hank pounded the end table, causing his gun to jitter slightly. A football match flickered on the screen. "That's more like it. You're excused." He waved me off, but as I turned to leave, he added, "Where's the other one?"

"Other one?" I echoed.

"You know damn well who I mean. Where's Wesley?"

That was exactly what I wanted to know—but was Hank just now noticing Wes's absence? My lips parted to speak when Wes answered from behind me.

"I'm right here. What do you want?"

I spun around, relieved to see Wes; I was so glad I could have kissed his cheek. He grinned back, his eyes wide in surprise.

"Where were you?" Hank demanded.

"Out working—where else? Somebody's got to bring home the bacon," Wes muttered.

Hank snorted, keeping his back turned. "You ought to buy a bag of goddamn chips with that bacon."

Wes frowned at me but quickly brushed off the expression as Hank turned in his seat to eye us. With a grunt, he returned to his game.

I grabbed Wes's arm and practically dragged him toward the kitchen.

"Damn, Eddie. I didn't realize you missed me that

much," he teased, snatching his arm from my grip.

"I gotta tell you something," I lowered my voice, checking over my shoulder for Hank. "The cops found a body this afternoon." I paused, waiting for a panicked reaction, but Wes simply blinked, urging me silently to continue.

"And?" he prompted.

I raised my eyebrows. "What if it's you-know-who?"

"Are you high?" he replied, squinting at me. "Just because the cops found a body doesn't mean it's *our* body." He punctuated his words with air quotes. "People die all the time, Eddie. It's probably just some junkie who overdosed. Why do you always work yourself up?" His tone was dismissive.

"Well, Coach Donahue called half an hour ago looking for Riley. What if Riley mentioned the cabin to them? We should go back and—"

"No," Wes exploded, glancing over his shoulder before leaning in close. "If we go back there, someone will discover something. Let's just act normal and forget about it. No one will ever find his car, anyway."

I hung my head, not daring to ask further, but needing to hear him say so. "You promise?"

"Hey. Look at me." He placed both hands on my shoulders. I peered into his face—our identical features, brown skin, narrow dark eyes, and thick coarse hair, though mine was tied back in a puffy ponytail while Wes sported low, neat sides with a curly top tipped reddish-blond. People often mistook us for pro basketball players. "What have I told you? No matter what happens, I'll always protect you, alright?" I nodded. "So trust me when I say no one will find out about Riley." He squeezed my shoulders firmly, easing some of my tension.

When he pulled away, I felt a small relief, yet I couldn't shake the worry. Mom used to say that even as a baby, she could tell my brain was always at work—observant, taking in every detail. That was how she could tell Wes and me apart.

"Okay. So where were you really? You got fired weeks ago. Hank is gonna kill you if he finds out," I jabbed him playfully.

Wes frowned and rolled his eyes. "Fuck that place. I've *really* been bringing home the bacon. Check this out," he said, rummaging in his pocket and pulling out two wads of twenty-dollar bills. "This one's your cut." He held out a roll.

My jaw dropped. "What the hell, Wesley? Where'd you get all that?" I sputtered, though my excitement quickly faded. "Wait—was that from the auto parts you stole?" I recalled the accusation from Wes's former manager at the auto shop.

"What? No. I didn't steal anything. Don't believe that

bullshit."

I gasped. "Well, is it *drug money* then?" Many kids at school had gotten mixed up with some mysterious guy called the Candy Man, a drug dealer. But Wes and I had sworn we'd never become that statistic. That's why we took up swimming.

"Damnit, Eddie." Wes spun around, eyes darting to ensure Hank wasn't listening. "Keep your voice down. And what difference does it make how I got it? It's in our hands and we damn well need it. Now take it." He forced the cash into my palm. "There's plenty left over after I pay the bills, so go buy yourself something nice. Haywood High's star swimmer deserves nothing but the best, right?"

"You're forgetting I'm second best, remember?"

"Bullshit. Riley's out of the picture now," he added bitterly.

"I wish you wouldn't say stuff like that," I whispered.

His brow arched. "Need I remind you what he was up to the other day?"

My chest deflated. "Please, don't." Neither of us wanted to relive that, and Brooklyn certainly didn't.

"Anyway," he waved his hand dismissively. "Just treat yourself—buy something nice, or even get Brooklyn a birthday present. She got you that expensive phone, didn't she? Do something special for her." He rolled his eyes. "Just enjoy yourself for once, damnit."

I shifted the wad of money to my other hand. "It's just…
doesn't any of this feel wrong to you?"

"Eddie—"

"No, not only that, but I could apply for a job too, you
know."

He scoffed. "Yeah, well, Hank made it crystal clear who
he expects to support this crumbling castle when he got me
that job." He rubbed at the scar across his brow—a
permanent reminder of when Hank smashed his face
through a glass table.

I gripped the wad, eyes lowering. "Maybe you should
put this away for next month's bills?" I pushed it toward
him.

Wes clicked his tongue and swatted my hand away.
"Eddie, there's plenty more where that came from."

"Do I even want to know what you mean by that?"

"I got a new job, okay? I crashed at Diego's until it came
through. If I couldn't replace the income, I probably
wouldn't have come back." He shrugged. "As you said,
Hank is gonna wreck me once he finds out they fired me.
But as long as cash is coming in, I figured I could stall him
a bit. This," he said, raising a fistful of bills, "is just a taste
of what's coming." He rolled his eyes. "Anyway, don't
worry about it. I'm a big boy."

I slowly grinned. "Well, big boy, I did your laundry

today." I motioned to the basket on the floor.

"Oh, wow. Thank you, Mom—" he froze mid-sentence. My smile faded, the image of that green top flashing through my mind. I started to ask him about it but thought better of it; Wes hated talking about Mom. "See," he added, eyeing the basket, "we're like the perfect pair. I work while you do the housework."

"Hey, men can take care of chores too. This isn't the fifties," I replied, giving him a playful shove and flipping my hair.

He dipped his head and chuckled. "Alright. But seriously, your job is to keep your grades up and dominate at the Spring Nationals next year. That's our ticket out of here." He gave my shoulder a poke.

He was right—the Spring Nationals *had* been the catalyst for everything. I hadn't always been on the swim team, which was why we'd committed the first crime.

3

EDDIE

THEN

I blinked at the bulletin board, my breath shallow. That was it—my second chance.

Before I could react, someone bumped my shoulder and then hooked an arm around my neck. "Is it fate or what?" Riley asked, jabbing a finger at the swim tryouts announcement.

"It sure as hell seems like it," I whispered back. Jackson, the team's butterfly swimmer in the medley relay, had transferred to Ridgedale, leaving us to replace him before next month's trials, which would decide who qualified for Nationals. The butterfly stroke was *my* specialty.

Riley squeezed me tighter. "You can't mess it up this

time, bro. We need you on the team." Riley, Wes, and Diego were already on board.

But I hadn't really screwed it up before—they had snatched the chance from me because of…

"Well, well, boys," Mr. Wright appeared beside Riley like the proverbial fly on the wall. I turned, jaw clenched.

Simon Wright, my foreign language and history teacher, was tall and lanky with brown hair brushed over his head, glasses, and a jutting chin. His soft, wispy voice always sent a chill down my spine.

He eyed me sideways. "Swim tryouts again, huh?" he remarked, exuding the unmistakable scent of a tuna sandwich.

Riley puffed his cheeks as though he were about to gag.

Thankfully, Mr. Wright reached into his pocket, producing a tin of breath mints. With a quick jerk, he knocked several into his mouth, crunching as he backed away.

"See you boys in class," he mumbled with his mouth full.

I stared at his receding figure until he vanished into his classroom. Something about the way he said that unsettled me.

A mere five minutes later, Mr. Wright reappeared, striding in front of the classroom. Of course, he paused at my desk—hence why I was forced to sit in the front row.

"Does anyone know what I just said?" he asked, blinking at me behind his black square glasses.

He uttered something in a foreign language, but it all sounded like gibberish to me.

Brooklyn raised her hand. "Guess what we're doing today? It's…"

"Uh-uh," he interrupted, waving a finger at her. "I want Edward to tell me which language it is."

I glared up at him, face flushing. What was his problem with me? My eyes darted briefly to Brooklyn before Mr. Wright lowered his gaze back to me. Shifting, I grumbled, "Italian?"

"Wrong." He slammed his hand down on my desk. "We covered this last week, Edward. Come on. Try again."

I sighed. "I don't recognize it, sir."

He straightened and motioned for Brooklyn to speak.

"It's French," she replied quietly, her eyes fixed on her lap.

"Correct. Maybe you two ought to be discussing that after school instead of playing hooky."

Some kids snickered.

"Maybe you should play sometime so you won't be so cranky," someone jeered from the back—I'm pretty sure it was Riley.

"Who said that?" Mr. Wright spun around.

"Your dick." That was definitely Diego, and everyone laughed, including me.

Mr. Wright joined in with a chuckle that grew so loud it hushed all our smiles, fading one by one. He staggered over to his desk, clutching his stomach dramatically. "You kids—you really crack me up." After catching his breath, he removed his glasses. "Since it's comedy hour, we're extending today's class by an extra thirty minutes."

Groans filled the room as his eyes landed on me while he cleaned his lenses with a handkerchief. "Oh, and Edward, you'll join me for after-school detention."

I jumped up. "I can't. The swim tryouts are at three o'clock."

"Well, I'm sorry, but you can't go. We need to work on your French. And if you don't take your seat, we'll be practicing French every day after school."

I slumped back into my seat, eyes stinging with tears. How dare Mr. Wright pull that shit on me again? Last spring I had missed the tryouts because he scheduled a meeting with Hank about my failing history test—and Hank had been livid. By the time the meeting ended, it was too late. Punctuality was one of Coach Donahue's biggest pet peeves.

I gritted my teeth and tried to focus on the chalkboard, struggling to stifle my sobs.

As Mr. Wright passed by, his soft voice trailed near my

ear, "Remember, Edward—I always have the last laugh…"

"That old fuck," Wes snarled at lunch later. "Who the hell does he think he is?"

I sighed, utterly exhausted from trying to figure out Mr. Wright's motives.

"Don't go," Wes said firmly.

I blinked at him. "What?"

"As captain of the swim team, I say skip detention and head to tryouts instead."

"Eddie, that could land you in more trouble," Brooklyn cautioned, squeezing my hand under the table.

April lobbed a piece of broccoli at Riley, giggling. "Did you really say that to Wright, though?" She tossed her braids over her shoulder.

Riley's expression darkened as he ran a hand through his brown hair. "I didn't think he'd take it out on you, Eddie. You didn't do anything wrong."

I shrugged. "It doesn't matter now. I'm never making the swim team if Wright's running the show."

Wes threw up his hands. "Why don't you just attend both tryouts and detention? You can show up late to detention. What's he gonna do—drag you out of the pool?"

"I wouldn't put it past him," I said grimly.

Wes rested his chin on his hand. "You know how much this means to us—making the team is our ticket out of here." He leaned closer. "It's our chance at freedom."

Didn't he think I already knew? Wes and I were top swimmers—Coach Donahue even said Wes had Olympic potential. *I* was faster than Wes. If winning Nationals meant getting noticed, I was in. I just couldn't stand another second in Haywood. Yet, Mr. Wright's shadow loomed large.

"I won't make the team. I refuse to see Wright's ugly face any longer than necessary." I looked at Wes. "I'm sorry."

We sat in silence for a moment, poking at our lunches, when Riley finally spoke. "Let's get even, then."

"What are you talking about?" Brooklyn demanded, turning to him sharply.

"I'm saying we get revenge on Wright."

"And how exactly are we doing that?" I asked.

Riley smiled slyly. "Meet me at my house at eight."

"I don't think I like this," Brooklyn whispered.

"Then butt out, Goody-Two-Shoes," Diego snapped. "It's your boyfriend's future on the line."

"That's not what I meant," Brooklyn whined, spinning to me. "You know I care about you. It's just…"

I nodded. "Brooklyn's right, guys. We shouldn't do anything that'll get us into more trouble."

Riley clicked his tongue. "You're all such amateurs. How will we get in trouble if he can't prove we did anything in the first place?"

Wes arched an eyebrow, then shrugged. "Okay. Fuck it. I'm in."

Diego nodded. "Me too."

April bobbed her head while wiping her lips with a napkin.

"April?" Brooklyn's eyes widened.

"*What?* I hate the bastard, and you all do too," April declared. "Besides, it's not like we're planning his murder or anything, right?" She glanced around at everyone.

Riley just smiled.

———

Later that evening, Wes, Diego, April, and I gathered on Riley's lawn at exactly eight. Brooklyn didn't show. I'd never been to the Donahues' place before—I hadn't expected it to be in such a rough neighborhood. At the corner, a gang of thugs argued rowdily; a couple of houses over, a front door stood wide open with a TV blasting at full volume, while a baby cried and nearby dogs howled. It was quite the cacophony for eight o'clock at night.

"Why are we all dressed in black?" I asked as I crunched on dried leaves approaching the crooked stoop. My eyes flicked to the boarded-up windows. Had Riley not jumped off the step, I'd never have believed anyone actually lived here.

"If you wore what you just had at school, you'd be digging your own grave," Riley replied.

"You idiot," Diego snickered, rolling his eyes. Diego was Latino, with reddish-brown curly hair and a freckled face that tempered his otherwise tough-guy image.

I folded my arms. "Why does what we're wearing matter? What exactly are we doing?"

"We're going to Wright's house," Riley said nonchalantly.

"*What?*" I choked out, eyes widening in disbelief.

"Damn!" Wes laughed.

"What if he's home?" I asked.

Riley shook his head. "He isn't."

"How do you know?"

"Every Thursday from five to ten, Wright spends time in the cancer ward with his wife," Riley explained.

"And how the hell do you know that?" April blurted out with a laugh before quieting as unease swept over us. "I—I'm sorry, Ri," she murmured softly.

I shot Riley a look, but he remained impassive. Everyone knew Mrs. Donahue—Riley's mother—had been undergoing chemo for the past month. How could April have forgotten?

Wes cleared his throat nervously. "So, are we doing this or what?"

"Yeah. Let's take my car," Riley replied. "Diego, your car

is too memorable.”

“I don’t want to leave my car here. Someone might steal it,” Diego muttered.

Riley sighed. “Trust me. They won’t. Everyone knows who my dad is, and they never mess with us.”

“Well, of course not. Nobody wants that piece of shit car anyway.” Diego pointed at the beat-up station wagon, and April giggled.

“Fine. Just park it in the garage. My dad isn’t home.” Riley’s cheeks flushed as he stormed off to his car.

Wes shot a look at Diego, who just shrugged. “Hey. My Charger is my baby.”

“How do you even know where Wright lives?” I asked Riley about ten minutes later.

He glanced at me through the rear-view mirror. “I found it online. There’s a website that can track anyone down if you have their full name. And get this: His name is Simon Dick Wright.”

We all laughed and started making puns for the rest of the ride.

Wright lived about twenty minutes from Riley’s place. We eventually pulled to a stop at the end of a narrow alley, our breathing anxious and heavy.

“Here, put these on,” Riley said, handing out masks that looked eerily similar to Michael Myers’. “In case he has security cameras," he added when I gave him a questioning look.

"Security cameras?" I echoed, my heart sinking.

Diego sighed. "He isn't *sure* there are cameras. We're just playing it safe."

"Also—no one is to say a word once we're inside," Riley instructed sharply.

"Why not?" April demanded, adjusting her mask. "Can we even breathe in these things?"

Riley sighed yet again. "Because, if there *are* cameras," he emphasized with a pointed look at me, "we don't want them picking up our voices."

"Right," Wes grinned. "All that'll show is five Michael Myers stalking around."

I lowered my gaze to the mask. Their plan was getting more and more ridiculous.

"Eddie, will you just grow a pair already?" Diego snapped, almost reading my mind. "You've missed two chances to join the swim team because of Wright. He deserves what's coming."

Wes bumped me reassuringly. "Look, if you'd rather wait in the car, that's fine."

"Hey..." Riley demanded our attention. "We're not going in there to vandalize or anything crazy. We're here to have a little fun." He reached under his seat and pulled out a stack of dirty magazines. "Let's give our favorite teacher a helping hand."

Unable to hold back, we all burst into laughter.

I raised my mask. "Let's do it."

We tried to exit the car as quietly as possible, yet every breath and scuff of our shoes echoed like a super-hearing nightmare. We parked behind the corner of the house, then slipped on our masks before following Riley to Wright's modest brick home with its white fence. I glanced back—there wasn't a soul in sight.

Wes fiddled with the padlock on the fence until, with no luck, he hopped over. One by one, the rest of us followed suit.

Riley knelt at the back door. "Bingo," he whispered, lifting a spare key from underneath the mat.

We crept through the dark kitchen. It was unnervingly cold, a fitting ambiance for Wright's icy lair.

Diego marched straight to the fridge. Using his hoodie sleeve, he flung the door open. I couldn't help but be curious about the contents inside, peeking into the bright light with my tongue practically holding the question.

Wright had meticulously labeled rows of brown paper bags and containers with each day of the week.

Diego shook his head as he reached for the bag labeled Friday. Calmly, he emptied the contents into the trash, then replaced the bag as if nothing was out of place.

Relaxing a bit, I chuckled and trailed along with Wes and Riley into the den. A lone lamp on the end table cast a dim orange glow over everything, and the stale smell hinted that the windows hadn't been opened in ages.

The furniture looked ancient, as though straight out of a seventies sitcom, and the gaudy floral wallpaper made me want to hurl.

Riley flipped to the middle of one magazine and dumped it on the coffee table. Diego set another atop the mantel between a white and gold candlestick set.

April and Wes had even removed a painting of horses to slip some torn pages inside the frame before re-hanging it on the wall.

If Wright didn't have cameras, what the hell would he make of all this upon discovering it?

***

Mr. Wright's gaze was stony when we walked into his classroom the following day. When we took our seats, he looked us each in the face, saying nothing.

I'D LOVE TO KNOW YOUR THOUGHTS

Reviews mean everything to an author. I would be really grateful if you could share your honest opinion about *Only the Pretty Ones* (it can be as short as you like.) And if you *did* enjoy *Only the Pretty Ones*, be sure to check out **nikikeith.com** for what's coming next.

I can't thank you enough for giving my book a chance. Take care! ☺

ABOUT THE AUTHOR

Niki Keith writes twisty young adult thrillers about broken teens doing bad things for all the right reasons. These days she prefers tea over coffee, dreams of going outer space, and is still searching for the best rice crispy recipe. When she isn't murdering fictional characters, she's cuddling with her affectionate love-biting kitty, pondering what to read next from her TBR pile.

You can connect with Niki on her website—nikikeith.com.

* 9 7 9 8 9 8 5 0 5 5 9 6 2 *